Devlin had a [barcode]
He had lost h

D0628384

"Let's start over." [...]
smoothly. "Pleased to meet you. The name's
Devlin Marlowe."

Lacey looked at his hand as if it were a rattlesnake.
"Maybe we should talk, Dev—"

"No," he said brusquely. "The past is the past. We
were kids. Life goes on."

He almost thought he saw a quick flare of hurt. He
started to drop his hand and tell her to forget the
whole thing—but then, very slowly, her hand rose
from her side and slid against his skin.

Dev felt as if someone had plowed a fist straight
into his gut. For one treacherous second, his mind
was filled with silvered moonlight on pale, smooth
skin, with hot, deep kisses and a longing he'd never
felt before—or since.

He closed his eyes so she wouldn't see how much
he wanted her.

Dear Reader,

Welcome back to Special Edition, where a month of spellbinding reading awaits you with a wonderful lineup of sophisticated, compelling August romances!

In bestselling author Jodi O'Donnell's memorable THAT'S MY BABY! story, *When Baby Was Born,* a pregnant woman with amnesia meets a cowboy she'll never forget! Beloved author Ginna Gray sweeps us away with another installment of her miniseries, A FAMILY BOND. In her emotional book *In Search of Dreams,* a woman with a scandalous past tries to say no to the man who vows to be in her future. Do you think a reunion that takes seventeen years to happen is worth waiting for? We're sure you'll say yes when you read *When Love Walks In,* Suzanne Carey's poignant story about a long-ago teenage passion that is rekindled—then a secret is exposed. When the hero of Carole Halston's *Because of the Twins...* needs help caring for his instant brood, the last thing he expects is a woman who turns his thoughts to matrimonial matters, too! Also this month is Jean Brashear's *Texas Royalty,* in which a tough, once-burned P.I. seeks revenge on the society girl who had betrayed him—until she manages to rekindle his desires *again!* And finally, Patricia McLinn kicks off her compelling new miniseries, A PLACE CALLED HOME, with *Lost-And-Found Groom,* about a treacherous hurricane that brings two people together for one passionate live-or-die night—then that remembered passion threatens to storm their emotional fortresses once and for all....

We hope you enjoy this book and the other unforgettable stories Special Edition is happy to bring you this month and all year long during Silhouette's 20th Anniversary celebration!

All the best,

Karen Taylor Richman
Senior Editor

JEAN BRASHEAR
TEXAS ROYALTY

Published by Silhouette Books

America's Publisher of Contemporary Romance

To Terry Acker, good friend and very first reader—
thanks for believing from that rough first effort
that this day would come

And to Penny Draeger, for her keen eye, generous heart
and constant encouragement—and for sharing
that fabulous stash of romance classics!

 SILHOUETTE BOOKS

ISBN 0-373-24343-X

TEXAS ROYALTY

Copyright © 2000 by Jean Brashear

Visit Silhouette at www.eHarlequin.com

Printed in U.S.A.

Books by Jean Brashear

Silhouette Special Edition

The Bodyguard's Bride #1206
A Family Secret #1266
Lonesome No More #1302
Texas Royalty #1343

JEAN BRASHEAR

A fifth-generation Texan, Jean Brashear hopes her forebears would be proud of her own leap into a new world. A lifelong avid reader, she decided when her last child was leaving the nest to try writing a book. The venture has led her in directions she never dreamed. She would tell you that she's had her heart in her throat more than once—but she's never felt more alive.

Her leap was rewarded when she sold her first novel, and her work has received much critical acclaim, including the Reviewers' Choice Award from *Romantic Times Magazine.* Happily married to her own hero, and the proud mother of two fascinating children, Jean is grateful for the chance to share her heartfelt belief that love has the power to change the world.

Jean loves to hear from readers. Send a SASE for reply to P.O. Box 40012, Georgetown, TX 78628 or find her on the internet via the Harlequin/Silhouette Web site at www.eHarlequin.com.

IT'S OUR 20th ANNIVERSARY!
We'll be celebrating all year,
Continuing with these fabulous titles,
On sale in August 2000.

Intimate Moments

#1021 A Game of Chance
Linda Howard

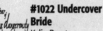
#1022 Undercover Bride
Kylie Brant

#1023 Blade's Lady
Fiona Brand

SECRETS! **#1024 Gabriel's Honor**
Barbara McCauley

#1025 The Lawman and the Lady
Pat Warren

#1026 Shotgun Bride
Leann Harris

Special Edition

#1339 When Baby Was Born
Jodi O'Donnell

#1340 In Search of Dreams
Ginna Gray

#1341 When Love Walks In
Suzanne Carey

#1342 Because of the Twins...
Carole Halston

#1343 Texas Royalty
Jean Brashear

#1344 Lost-and-Found Groom
Patricia McLinn

Desire

MAN OF THE MONTH **#1309 The Return of Adams Cade**
BJ James

#1310 Tallchief: The Homecoming
Cait London

#1311 Bride of Fortune
Leanne Banks

#1312 The Last Santini Virgin
Maureen Child

TEXAS GROOMS **#1313 In Name Only**
Peggy Moreland

#1314 One Snowbound Weekend...
Christy Lockhart

Romance

#1462 Those Matchmaking Babies
Marie Ferrarella

#1463 Cherish the Boss
Judy Christenberry

#1464 First Time, Forever
Cara Colter

#1465 The Prince's Bride-To-Be
Valerie Parv

#1466 In Want of a Wife
Arlene James

#1467 His, Hers...Ours?
Natalie Patrick

Prologue

Houston, Texas
Seventeen years ago

Moonlight drifted over her skin like the kiss of a lover. Devlin's hands weren't quite steady as they traced Lacey's tender curves. With a reverence he hadn't expected to feel, he brushed his lips against hers.

When Lacey gasped softly and tightened slender fingers in his hair, every last vestige of Dev's desire for revenge flew away. Who her father was and how much Dev hated him didn't matter anymore. All that mattered was that after this night, they would be forever changed. Forever bound.

"Dev?" Her voice trembled as his hands had.

"Shh, it's all right. You're so beautiful, Lacey."
At eighteen, his experience was not vast, but it was
far greater than hers. He smiled, rewarded by the
answering curve of hers, that lush, full mouth that
drove him crazy.

"You're the one who's beautiful." She trailed
her fingers across his chest, and Dev thought he
might die of pleasure.

"I'm a guy. I can't be beautiful," he protested.

She laughed faintly. "Shows what you know. If
you could see yourself like I see you—"

He wanted to ask what she saw, this girl who
had everything, whose father kept Devlin's family
in thrall like some sort of feudal king held his serfs.
But he didn't really want to know—not tonight,
when she was heaven in his arms. All that mattered
tonight was that she wanted him—enough to make
him her first. Her last, if he had anything to say
about it.

"Dev?"

He paused, looking solemnly into her wide, innocent silvery eyes. "Are you sure about this?"

He could see the pulse beating in her throat. He
could see the tiny fleck of fear. His heart sank, but
this was too important—*she* was too important—to
rush.

Then she smiled, and the tiny fleck vanished.
"I'm only afraid because I don't know what to do.
I want it to be you, Dev. Only you."

His throat tightened. Lacey DeMille, the River
Oaks princess, wanted Devlin Marlowe, the kid
from the wrong side of the tracks. Dev kissed her
with all the wonder he felt. Then he sat back on his

heels in the moon-silvered gazebo and imprinted her on his memory for eternity—the girl he would never forget.

Lacey reached for him, and he bent to press another kiss as his hands began to unbutton his jeans—

"Lacey, is that you?" her father called out. "Is someone with you?"

The magic shattered under harsh, blinding light.

"What the hell do you think you're doing?" Charles DeMille's voice fractured the night, bludgeoning its beauty with jagged, angry blows.

Lacey screamed, shrinking back from the flashlight's glare, wrapping her arms around her body.

Dev grabbed his T-shirt and slipped it over her head. He turned, standing in front of her to protect her.

Her father knocked him to the ground with a roar of rage. "You worthless piece of trash—I told you to stay away from her. Who do you think you are, putting your filthy hands on my daughter?"

Dev jumped up to defend Lacey, but she scampered away from his touch as though it were poison. He tried to catch her gaze, but she was sobbing hysterically and grasping for her clothes.

"You can't do this. Lacey and I—we're in love." Defiantly, Dev faced his nemesis.

"Love!" Charles DeMille's laughter was a harsh bark. "You're not fit to lick her boots."

Dev waited for Lacey to speak up, to tell her father that it was true, that she loved him as he loved her. But she didn't look at him, didn't say a word. "Tell him, Lacey. We're going to be together. Come with me now, tonight. I'll take care of you, I swear I will.''

But Lacey only looked frightened.

Her father laughed at Dev as he had for three years, ever since the night Dev's father had died in disgrace and everything had changed. ''You can't even take care of the family you have, can you, son? You'll never amount to anything, and you damn sure won't ever get near my daughter again. I'll kill you if you try.''

Dev stared at the ground then, his mind roaring with rage at being humiliated in front of Lacey. He'd tried to care for his family, but DeMille held all the cards.

''Get back to the house, Lacey,'' her father ordered.

She turned away, a look on her face so wounded that Dev felt her pain himself. ''Lacey—'' he called out, hating himself for not being able to beat Charles DeMille, almost hating her for denying what was between them.

And then she was gone.

Dev's chin jutted out. He would not show this man fear. This man had savaged his pride too hard, too often.

''First thing tomorrow, you are joining the military. You'll be on the first bus to basic training.''

''I won't leave her.''

Clipped tones answered him. ''If I'd known she was sneaking around to meet you, you'd already be gone. You'd better thank your lucky stars I caught you when I did.''

Dev wanted to hurt him. "How do you know it was the first time?"

His jaw stung from the force of DeMille's blow, but Dev stood his ground. The man leaned right in Dev's face, smelling of expensive Scotch and smuggled cigars.

"You will leave, or you'll go to jail. Lacey's underage, or hadn't you thought about that?"

"My family—" What would they do?

"Maybe you should have thought about them before." DeMille shoved a finger in Dev's chest. "You aren't calling the shots here, boy. I am. You won't be much good to your family if you're in prison. This way, you're only gone for two years— unless you get wise and sign up for more."

Dev refused to drop his stare, but he knew he was defeated. DeMille had the power. Dev was afraid of what another disgrace would do to his mother. She'd been drowning herself in drink for three years. But his sisters and kid brother—what would happen to them without him?

He summoned every ounce of strength within him and met DeMille's stare with equal force. "I want your promise that my family won't pay for this. They'll pay enough, just having me gone."

Oddly enough, though he hated DeMille, Dev knew his word was good on this one thing. He had never understood why his father's old boss had stepped in when their world had fallen apart—or why Dev's mother had let him.

Dev hated being a charity case, hated what they'd become, hated it that his mother had faith in

DeMille but not in him. The family was Dev's responsibility, not DeMille's.

DeMille nodded sharply. "You're the only bad apple in the bunch, Devlin. I'll take care of them. And if you're wise, you'll stay gone a long time. Just write your mother so she doesn't worry."

Dev would leave, because he had no choice. But it wouldn't always be like this.

He had to make certain of one more thing. Though her abandonment cut him to the bone, Dev had to know that Lacey wouldn't suffer. "What about Lacey?"

DeMille snorted. "I know who's at fault here. I'll give her everything you could never provide."

Dev's pride demanded its due. "You're wrong. I love her. I can take care of her."

Charles DeMille just shook his head. "Your father was headed for prison when he died. You think you'll ever be good enough for my daughter?" He clapped Dev on the shoulder, smug that he had won. "Son, you're nothing. You never were."

Then his face turned harsh again. "Now get out of here before I change my mind and call the cops."

Chapter One

Present Day

Devlin Marlowe entered the ballroom late, pausing at the entrance and surveying the crush of people. Houston glitterati had turned out in force. If the women assembled had merely donated the price of their designer gowns and gleaming jewels, no auction would be needed to raise funds.

He could afford the price of admission now, thanks to a series of shrewd investments, but beneath his skin, he still didn't belong with these people. He might own his own tux, but inside him still lived the boy who'd barely escaped going on welfare.

This occasion gave him a golden chance to do

what he wanted—to observe Lacey DeMille at close range before she saw him.

And he wanted that, he realized. Wanted time to assess her in the flesh. Wanted to see if there was anything left of the beautiful young girl he had wanted so badly to choose him.

Before he tore her life apart, he wanted to find the right way to handle it. He owed it to the Gallaghers. They had become more than clients—they were friends he didn't want to see hurt.

But fate must be laughing up its sleeve at him. Dev sure wasn't.

Even though he'd done all the investigating himself, a part of him still didn't want to believe what he'd found.

Out of all the women in the world, what kind of loser luck had him turning up the Princess of River Oaks as the missing baby girl a family had hired him to find?

This wasn't personal. He couldn't let it be. Nothing he did could regain the lost years, could repair the awful sense of impotence…of teetering on the brink…of being one of the nameless, faceless poor after his family's precipitous fall from grace when his father suffered a fatal heart attack, one step away from being jailed for fraud.

They'd held onto their dignity with white-knuckled hands. But Dev still remembered all too well the nights the scared boy he'd once been had dug claws into his sides to keep from giving in to unmanly sobs. The angry teenager who had fought Charles DeMille's disdain, his hold on Dev's mother. The young lover whose perfect revenge had turned into his worst defeat.

The man he was now knew that he'd been forged in the fire of his family's needs. He'd served his time in the military and come back to take them away to Dallas. He'd worked hard, two and sometimes three jobs, to support them. He'd built a business and made it successful. He'd found his way on his own and was better off for it.

All that was in the past. This was a job, a special duty for valued friends. Reuniting a woman with siblings she didn't know she had. He would do it as cleanly as possible, and then go to the next case.

Lacey's adoption had been done by less-than-legal means and covered up in a way only money and power could manage. Charles DeMille had plenty of both.

It was easy now to see why no one had known. Dev was almost certain that even Lacey had no idea she was adopted—the girl who had walked away because he wasn't good enough for her blue blood. The girl who had betrayed him, who had chosen a life of ease over his love. Who had taught him a lesson so painful he remembered it still.

It was too rich that Devlin Marlowe would be the one to tell her that her blood was no better than his.

What a tangled web we weave, when first we practice to deceive… Lacey DeMille's whole life was defined by her parents' lies. She stood on quicksand and didn't even know it.

Sleeping Beauty was about to be awakened, one way or another.

But not with a kiss.

And no one had ever called Devlin Marlowe a prince.

Lacey stood with her date, Philip Forrester, and her parents, watching the auction as though she'd had no part in creating it. Her mind drifted to Christina, the little girl for whom she volunteered as a child advocate. To the contrasts between their lives…her own so privileged, so unearned.

The demands of that life sometimes choked Lacey. A part of her wanted so much to care nothing about how she looked or behaved, to run free like a ruffian and just be Lacey, not Lacey of the River Oaks DeMilles.

From her earliest days, she had known she must not. Although it was never said aloud, she had always known that she was held to a higher standard. That she had to be very careful not to slip.

But though she sometimes chafed at the propriety required, she loved her parents deeply and knew they loved her. It was bedrock. She was a DeMille.

"Agnes is pleased with your handling of the gala," her mother, Margaret, murmured.

Her mother's friend Agnes was a tyrant, but Lacey merely smiled. "I think things are going well." It all seemed so superficial, after what she'd seen today—but the funds she raised would go to the Child Advocacy Center.

"You and Philip will drop by our little gathering week after next?"

"Little gathering" didn't quite do justice to Margaret's annual cocktail reception for four hundred, held the night before a hospital fund-raiser. "Certainly," Lacey responded. "Wouldn't miss it."

"You make a lovely couple."

Of course they did. Margaret had handpicked Philip as her latest bid for Lacey to marry and settle down to raise the next generation of DeMilles. A prominent young plastic surgeon with blue blood of his own, suave blond Philip Forrester was considered quite a catch.

Except by her. She couldn't seem to convince her parents that they wouldn't marry.

"Lacey, are you all right?" Philip asked.

"What?" She stirred. Around them the crowd buzzed, and Lacey realized that her item had been called as next up for bidding. "Oh—yes. Just fine."

Philip leaned down and whispered, "So where shall I take this fabulous picnic you're auctioning? Will you actually prepare it with your own hands?"

Lacey met his smile with one of her own. "You'd like it better if I let Clarise do the cooking."

Philip nodded in agreement. "You don't need to learn to cook. We'll have our own servants."

"Philip, we aren't—" He, like everyone else, assumed.

His glance grazed her. "Please, Lacey. Not tonight."

There was nothing wrong with Philip. He was well-set financially, with a successful career and family money behind him. Impeccable manners, moved through the upper crust with aplomb, treated Lacey like a princess, but—

But what? What was she waiting for? She'd been

through a number of beaux, had received her share of proposals from men her parents considered eminently suitable. She had accepted none. They all wanted what she brought to the table, not who she was.

She wanted something no one had offered. To be loved for herself, not her money or social position. To be loved deeply for who she was inside. Maybe she was a hopeless romantic, but Lacey had dug in her heels over this one requirement.

She'd been foolish twice, been impetuous and learned hard lessons. She would never again fall for a charming rogue. But she wanted that one great love, that grand passion.

Just then her father winked at her. "Want me to run up the bid, princess?"

Lacey smiled and shook her head, rousing herself to tune into the bidding. Around her, discreet gestures raised the price by fifty or a hundred dollars.

"Fifteen hundred," the auctioneer called, nodding toward Philip's faint signal. "Do I have sixteen?"

A brief pause of silence.

The auctioneer scanned the crowd. "All right. A gourmet picnic for four provided by Lacey DeMille going once...twice—

"Two thousand," came a voice from the back.

Lacey felt it like an electric shock. Who would do such— Around her, the crowd stirred. She couldn't see over them to find the owner of the voice.

"Well, Ms. DeMille has not only created a marvelous occasion, but it appears that she'll garner the highest contribution yet. Further bids?''

Philip glanced down at her, eyebrows lifted.

Lacey shook her head. ''You don't need to up the ante.'' She was well aware that he was only here for appearances.

''Two thousand going once…going twice…''

Philip glanced across the crowd and frowned. ''Twenty-one hundred.''

''Three thousand.'' Same voice.

Lacey resisted the urge to stand on tiptoe. Around her, heads were craning to see the persistent bidder.

The auctioneer looked straight at Philip. ''Do I have thirty-five hundred?''

She knew that Philip's sense of thrift was screaming. He could easily afford it, but he considered economy a prime virtue. And this was her cause, not his. He didn't like her choice of volunteer work. Like her parents, he thought she should be doing something more antiseptic.

After a long pause, he nodded, jaw clenched.

''Thirty-five hundred. Do I hear four thousand?''

The crowd fell silent. Expectation vibrated the air around them. Lacey wanted to slink out of the room as fervid glances darted her way.

''Who is it?'' she whispered to Philip.

''I don't know.'' His eyes narrowed. ''I can't see where he is.''

Lacey cast a glance over at her mother, whose face had gone stiff. Public spectacles were not part of the family code. Lacey had been on the receiving end of that reproof too often. Old South to the core,

Margaret had a rigid code of behavior that her daughter had spent her life trying to meet. In this very modern age, Margaret stood for a way of life that had almost vanished. She'd fight for it with her dying breath.

Lacey rubbed one hand across her stomach and took another deep breath. Part of her wanted to push through the crowd and find the man who didn't understand that such things weren't done. Part of her wanted to hide.

The pause went on long enough that she thought she was safe, that Philip would win, though she had no doubt how much he'd hate paying the price for a picnic he could have just by asking.

"Going...going—"

"Five thousand." The voice rang out in deep, decisive tones.

Around them the buzz rose. Her father was staring at Philip, waiting for him to take the lead.

She could see on his face that though pride was involved, pride would only take him so far.

The auctioneer stared at Philip.

Lacey held her breath.

Finally, Philip shook his head.

"Five thousand it is—a record for this event. Five thousand dollars for a gourmet picnic for four provided by our own Lacey DeMille."

Around them clapping began, along with curious looks. Missy Delavant leaned across Philip with a stage whisper. "Did you get a look at him, Lacey? Do you have something going that we need to know about?"

Lacey recoiled from the woman who'd give anything to get her hooks into Philip. "I haven't seen—I have no idea who it is." She drew herself up in her best Margaret imitation. "If you'll excuse me, I have to check on some details."

She cast Philip a glance, seeing disapproval written on his face. A glance at her mother revealed a mirror image. Her father's eyebrows lifted in surprise.

The burning in her stomach returned.

Lacey stood very straight and moved toward the front of the room.

Just shy of her destination, a man stepped out of the crowd and blocked her path.

"Hello, Lacey. Long time no see."

Dev looked down into silvery eyes he'd thought never to see again. Fragile. He hadn't expected fragile, but she looked like a doe caught by surprise, a sylph poised to melt away in the mists of the forest.

She was beautiful. More beautiful than ever. The woman had more than fulfilled the promise of the girl. Dressed in a fall of lavender silk, she wore a slender silver ribbon at her throat, an amethyst pendant glowing against skin pale as camellias. Or white satin.

And he wanted her again. Wanted her still.

Damn.

She had betrayed him. Had chosen comfort and luxury over love. Had walked away from him without a backward glance and chosen Daddy's money. Daddy's approval.

"Dev?"

Those eyes. Her sister's eyes, he saw now. Silver, with the black ring around the iris. No wonder he'd felt Maddie Gallagher's draw when he'd first met her, though it would never have occurred to him to make a connection then. Their hair was the same chestnut, though Lacey's was a short, gamine cut feathering around her delicate features. Maddie's was long and wild, in tune with her earthy exuberance.

For a moment, Lacey looked almost...vulnerable. *Don't be vulnerable, Lacey. I have news that's going to shatter your world. You have to be strong.*

"Is it really you?" she asked.

That mouth. That impossibly lush mouth, fit more for a courtesan than a Junior Leaguer. It was the other feature she shared with Maddie—and the irony struck him. He'd seen Boone Gallagher's brain turned to mush more than once by that mouth. He'd been amused.

He was amused no longer.

"Yeah." He spoke, finally. But his voice was rusty. Hoarse. "It's me."

It's a job, Dev. Just a job. Forget the past. It will only make things worse.

So he grinned to cover the rawness he hadn't expected to feel. "How are you?"

"Why are you here, Dev?"

The implication that he was out of place stung. Anger rode to his rescue. "Don't worry—I can afford the price of admission now."

For a fleeting instant, he thought he saw shame

flicker in her eyes, but it was gone so quickly, he could easily have imagined it.

When silver eyes turned to frost, he knew he had. "If you'll excuse me, I have to take care of my donation. It was nice seeing you again, Dev," she said, as if he were just a casual acquaintance.

As if he'd never seen her naked. Or heard her moan into his kiss.

She turned to go, and Dev's hand shot out to stop her.

Lacey stepped away from him before he could touch her. One eyebrow tilted in his direction. Her look was one of a princess to peasant. You dare to touch me? it said.

Dev nearly lost it then. "Not so fast, Ms. De-Mille."

She glanced in the direction of the perfectly groomed blond he'd seen her with earlier. The man was exactly her type, and it made Dev burn.

"Yes?" Her shoulders stiffened, just a fraction. They were too slender, if intimidation was the effect she wanted.

And for a moment, Dev felt a crazy urge to protect her from what must come.

Then her mother looked out at him through Lacey's eyes. Margaret DeMille, with all her Southern propriety and perfect manners, might not be Lacey's blood mother, but she had molded Lacey in all the ways that counted, down to the way she'd taught her daughter to look down her nose, even though Dev was half a foot taller.

And fury shot through his veins. Fury for all the lost years, for all the suffering. For Charles De-

Mille's contempt for Dev's efforts to protect his family—and for telling Dev to keep his filthy hands off DeMille's precious daughter. Fury for laying his heart at this woman's feet and having her turn away as if he'd offered something dirty and unworthy.

And fury made him rough. "We have a date to set, Ms. DeMille."

That got to her. Shock rippled across the too-perfect features. "What?"

At last, Dev got a little taste of revenge. "I bought you."

Her eyes closed, then flew open again. "You," she accused. "It was you."

He smiled with satisfaction. The look on her face was worth every penny. "Yeah. It was me." He wouldn't charge the Gallaghers for his exorbitant bid. This one was on him.

She was something to behold, all right. Dev watched her struggle to cover her shock and dismay with those perfect, elegant manners. And if something about her struggle twisted something inside his chest, at least he had a measure of satisfaction for all that he and his family had suffered. It was a long way from justice, but it would have to do. He had a job to complete, and he couldn't make this personal.

"Very well." She had it all back now, every feature composed, the slate wiped clean as if he were a total stranger. "If you'll give me your card, I'll call to make arrangements to be available when it's most convenient for you and your friends."

"There will only be two of us. And I'd better call you. I live in Dallas now, and I travel a lot.

What's your number?'' Though he already had it. Unlisted numbers were little challenge for a private investigator.

When she gave him a cell phone number instead, he resisted the urge to counter with her home number just to rattle her.

"Do you need a piece of paper?'' she asked.

"No.'' He caught her gaze, full on. "I have an excellent memory.''

For a moment, shadows darkened her eyes, but she recovered quickly. "Fine. Does your guest have any dietary restrictions?''

Oh, Lacey. You make it too easy.

"I don't know,'' he replied, grinning in anticipation. "You tell me.''

A tiny frown appeared between her brows, but he saw the moment she understood his meaning. Saw her shrink back the tiniest fraction. "Oh, no. That won't be possible.''

"It's a worthy cause, right? I'd hate to have to withdraw my bid. There was no mention that I couldn't pick my own guests.''

This time the struggle wasn't so easily mastered. For a moment, Dev wished he could rewind and try this again. Figure out another way. Wished he could kill the need that even now, after what she'd done, made his body crave hers.

She swallowed hard and shook her head. "No. There wasn't.'' She lifted her head, and he was surprised to find himself proud of her strength. "Dev, if this is about what hap—''

He broke in. "No, Lacey. The past is the past. No point in rehashing. It doesn't have anything to do with who we are now.'' It couldn't. Wouldn't. Not anymore. Too much was at stake.

Confusion swirled in her gaze, and he cursed himself silently. He'd lost his cool. It couldn't happen again. ''Let's start all over.'' He held out his hand. ''Ms. DeMille, pleased to meet you. The name's Devlin Marlowe.''

She looked at his hand as if it were a rattlesnake, poised to strike. Then she glanced back up at him, and he wished he knew what she was thinking. ''Maybe we should talk, Dev—''

''No.'' If he knew one thing, it was that nothing was to be gained by digging into their past. She had too much ahead of her to deal with, and he had to keep his emotions in check. ''It was nothing. We were kids. Life goes on.''

He almost thought he saw a quick flare of hurt. He started to drop his hand and tell her to forget the whole thing—but then, very slowly, her hand rose from her side and slid against his skin.

And Dev felt as though someone had plowed a fist straight into his gut.

For one treacherous second, his mind was filled with silvered moonlight on pale, smooth skin. With hot, deep kisses and a longing he'd never felt before—or since.

It was all Dev could do not to drop her hand like a hot potato, but instead, he even surprised himself. He drew her hand up to his lips. He breathed in her scent, redolent of spices and tropical flowers, and he closed his eyes so she wouldn't see how much he wanted her. How much memory claimed him. How much she had the power to hurt him.

Still.

He pressed his mouth to her knuckles and heard her tiny gasp.

Then he let her go and summoned the strength to smile like nothing mattered.

"I know you want to back out. I hope you won't." He waited a beat. "The decision is yours. I'll call you."

Then he walked away, feeling as if he'd just stepped back from the edge of a very steep cliff.

He was not dashing his body on the rocks for Lacey DeMille again.

Chapter Two

In a packed ballroom almost steamy with the heat of many bodies, Lacey shivered as she watched him walk away.

But her palm was hot where he had touched her, and on her knuckles she could feel the imprint of his mouth. Her body quivered with the lightning bolt that had arced from his body to hers.

And she didn't know whether to laugh or cry or scream that Devlin Marlowe had walked back into her life.

"Lacey, darling, who is that man and why is he here?" Her mother's voice grated across nerves already strained past bearing. Then Philip walked up to her other side and turned her toward him.

"Is that him?" he demanded. "The one who—"

Bought me? Lacey fought a laugh wrenched up

from the rawness within her, remembering Dev's bold statement. He had been like that then, full of daring and mischief. He had made her want to be like him, so unafraid, so ready to take on anything. Anyone.

Come with me now, tonight. I'll take care of you, I swear I will. Words she'd buried deep rose to the surface and taunted. Lacey bit her lip to stem tears she couldn't explain.

Why, Dev? Why did you leave?

She hadn't believed her father at first, but when Dev never even checked to see if she was all right after that horrible night, she'd known the truth.

Lust at first sight, a youthful impulse—and a painful mistake.

Dev had asked her to go away with him that night, not seeing how impossible it was. Her father would have hunted them to the ends of the earth. She'd been packed off to school in Europe, her heart in tatters. Foolish little girl.

Lacey had been a fool not once, but twice. She didn't want to hurt like that ever again. She was always careful now.

"What's wrong? What did he say to you?" Philip demanded. "He is the one, isn't he?"

"I can't believe he made such a spectacle," her mother complained. "I hope you set him straight and canceled that ridiculous arrangement."

Lacey was drowning in voices, in demands. All she wanted was to be alone, to go someplace quiet where she could try to absorb what had happened.

"Lacey?" Philip's hand was on her elbow. "What's wrong with you?"

She did laugh then, one short burst, quickly stifled. Her mother and Philip stared at her as though she'd lost her mind.

And another laugh leaked out of her, then grew stronger. Soon she was laughing hard enough that it seemed reasonable that tears would escape and roll off her lashes.

"That's it," Philip grated. "I'm taking you home."

"I'll call Dr. Byrne," her mother offered. "He'll prescribe something to settle your nerves."

Lacey wiped her eyes and tried to compose herself to answer, but before she could, her father had intervened.

"She doesn't need a doctor, Margaret. I'll take care of this." He pulled her to the side and shot back an order. "Go get her a glass of water, Philip."

Her father led her away from the crowd looking on with avid glances. When they were at the edge of the room, he turned her to face him, his expression stern.

"That was Marlowe, wasn't it?" He didn't have to say the name. "Was he the bidder?"

Lacey could only nod. Memories held her fast in their grip. She felt almost as naked now as she had that night.

"What did you tell him?"

Nothing seemed real. Not her father standing in front of her, not her mother's horror, not Philip's presumption. Not the touch she could still feel on her skin. Or the green eyes that could still claim her.

"It will be fine, Daddy. I can handle it."

"You're going to do this?" His voice rose, and the little girl she'd been shrank from his disapproval. "I forbid it. I'll take care of this, Lacey. He won't bother you again."

Just like her father had taken care of her other mistake, obtaining an annulment and hushing up her ill-fated elopement. He had the connections to do it.

He'd been right, of course. She and Luc could never have made it. They were too different—and that, of course, was the attraction. He was a race car driver she met during her last year in Europe. A reprobate, a bad boy all the way, he had made her blood run hot. Just like Dev.

He'd made her want to dare things she shouldn't. Just like Dev.

Then he had taken her father's money and vanished like smoke.

Just like Dev.

It doesn't have anything to do with who we are now.

Was Dev right?

Her heart said no. And she couldn't, wouldn't make another mistake. She knew nothing about this Dev, only that a boy bearing his name had taught her about passion—and then walked away without a backward glance.

She should let her father handle it. Only he knew what had happened. Only he knew how little Dev had cared. He would handle it, and she would never have to see Devlin Marlowe again.

The decision is yours. Dev gave her more credit than her own family did.

Within Lacey arose something she couldn't name. Some tiny seed of all her wondering why she was here, what her life meant.

"No, Daddy." She lifted her gaze to his and parroted Dev's words. "It was a long time ago. We were just kids. He can't hurt me now."

"Princess, you're wrong." His voice carried too much force for something so far removed.

"Don't worry, Daddy. I know you want to protect me, but I'll be fine, I promise."

"No, princess. Don't do it."

"Why not?" She was honestly curious. "I'm not sixteen. I made my mistakes with Dev, with Luc. But I'm a grown woman now. You have to let me handle it."

She could see a war going on behind his eyes. "Daddy, it's just a picnic. It's for the children."

Her father's frown deepened and he started to speak but then shook his head. "I wish you wouldn't."

"Is there something I should know?"

Her father glanced away for a second, then returned his gaze to hers. Finally, he shook his head slowly, exhaling in a gust. "No. There's nothing. Just be careful, princess. Be very careful."

She smiled then, to ease his mind. "It's only a picnic, Daddy. I can handle it."

She prayed she was right.

Dev leaned against the window frame and stared into the dark night outside his hotel room, unseeing.

He swore a few choice, ripe curses, raked his fingers through his hair and shoved away from the wall to return to the desk where his laptop accused him.

The cursor blinked patiently, waiting for Dev to organize his thoughts. But all he could see was a pair of silvery eyes gone icy and imperious. Was there even a trace of soft gray velvet left inside that perfectly groomed exterior?

Just a job. It's just a job. You're not a kid anymore, and neither is she.

Yanking his tuxedo shirt out of the waistband of his slacks, Dev worked at the studs, stripping the garment off his body and tossing it on the bed. Then he sat down again and used the discipline that had marked his life for years to focus on the screen before him. He knew the facts of the case; he could relate them to Lacey, carefully and with no emotion at all. That would be the best way. Just the facts, ma'am.

If only it were that simple.

Right now, he'd like to talk to Maddie. He could use a reminder of all the reasons this case had nothing to do with him. But it was two-thirty in the morning, and the Gallaghers rose with the chickens.

And all he'd told Mitch and Boone and Maddie was that he knew who Lacey was, not all that had gone on between them years ago. If he thought the words on the screen made a long, complicated story, try adding in his own little tangent.

Okay. How would he start? *Lacey, there's this tiny town called Morning Star, where a man named*

Dalton Wheeler took the rap for a murder he didn't commit—

Dev shook his head. Okay— *There was a girl named Jenny who loved Dalton very much, but he vanished and she found out she was pregnant and she went away to have you and had to give you up.*

Damn. It was all true, as far as it went. But how to explain to her about all the love, the heartache?

Would Lacey understand that in those days, Jenny had few options? She went away, had the baby, and the doctor took care of the adoption. Jenny never knew about the very wealthy man and his wife who staged an elaborate deception because bloodlines were so important. Margaret DeMille would never admit that the child she ostensibly went to the pure country air of Switzerland to have was not her own. That the baby girl was tiny and delicate only helped in disguising her true age when they returned to Houston.

So they told no one, not even Lacey. She slept tonight, wrapped up in her certainty of who she was, where she belonged.

And he prowled a hotel room and wished for sleep. He should have stayed at his brother's. At least Connor would distract him from thoughts he didn't welcome.

They're good people, Lacey. Give them a chance. Don't get on your high horse and break their hearts.

Hell, maybe Maddie was the right person to tell her.

No. It was his job. He always did his job. Even if he trusted the Ice Princess not to hurt Maddie—

which he didn't—he had never skipped out on a job and he wouldn't start now.

Dev cursed softly. He wasn't going to sleep tonight. Dallas was only three hours away, and he had other cases, other commitments. With quick, decisive steps, he changed into jeans and packed up. Maybe in his own bed, he could stop the thoughts whirling long enough to get a little shut-eye. Then he'd make a game plan.

In his '78 Caddy gas guzzler that rode like a living room sofa, Dev took a detour on his way out of town. He drove down River Oaks Boulevard with its grand homes shrouded in trees. Lacey didn't live at the estate anymore—she had her own condo not far away—but he wanted to take a look at his enemy's lair.

There it was, down the long circular drive. Two-story colonial with mahogany front doors, the wide front porch opening out onto manicured grounds. Huge pines and magnolias scattered over emerald lawn, thickening stands of them at the boundaries. In the spring the azaleas would scatter brilliant bursts of color. From the street, the whole place looked like a dream house.

Appearances could be so deceptive. Somewhere, nestled way back under the trees, was the gazebo where dreams had died.

Cursing softly, Dev pulled away. A few blocks farther, he stopped in front of a condo where he knew there was a jazzy red convertible in the garage. He looked at the darkened windows and wondered which ones let moonlight filter onto her bed.

He remembered a gazebo silvered in moon glow.

Remembered innocent gray velvet eyes. Silken curves trembling under his hands.

What are you dreaming tonight, Lacey?

Dev set his jaw, sipped at the paper cup of coffee and drove away.

Lacey awoke from a fitful sleep and glanced at the clock. Three-fifteen. The headlights from a passing car swept across the wall. She rolled over and stared across the lavender silk comforter toward the moonlight spilling into her window, drifting across her shoulder.

You're so beautiful, Lacey. She couldn't have seen the green of his eyes that long-ago night, so serious and dark as he bent over and unfastened the bodice of her dress, but somehow they were always that startling green in her dreams. He had taught her the hum of rapture beneath the boundaries of her skin. Had sent the heat of ecstasy rushing through her veins.

Are you sure about this? Had she been sure? Or just so full of her pipe dreams that she couldn't see how they had been doomed from the start?

Somehow tonight after seeing Dev again, she could remember, for the first time in years, not how badly it had ended, not the shouts, the fear, the awful nakedness.

Instead, she remembered nerves. Jive-jumpy thrill, pounding in her blood. The sweetness of an ache that had stolen her breath. Longing so sharp she could taste it still. Everything with Dev had seemed larger than life. More colorful. More intense.

Intense. That was Dev then—and now. She'd seen the fierce glow still inside him tonight.

She had fallen headlong into the madness, trusting Devlin Marlowe to be her first, the one she would remember forever. The man who would make her a woman. He would be her one true love. She'd been so sure.

Foolish, foolish girl. Tears slipped across her temple and trickled into her hair as Lacey watched the moon slide behind whispery clouds.

Silly little rich girl. Lacey wept for the innocent and her fanciful dreams....

The girl who never suspected that even love had its price.

Ringing woke her into sunlight that sliced into her vision. Lacey tripped on the edge of the comforter and fumbled for the cell phone in her purse. She squeezed her lids shut against the glaring brightness. "Hello?" she croaked.

"Too early?"

She glanced at the clock but couldn't make out the numbers. "What time is it?"

"Nine-thirty."

She groaned, then bolted up straight. "Dev?"

"Not a morning person, right?" His tone was dry.

"No, it's just—" She swallowed hard and threw her shoulders back, standing up straight, as if military posture might help. "Never mind. Why did you call?"

His tone went brisk and impersonal. "I have to

be in Dallas all week. I'd like to schedule the picnic
for next Saturday. Will that work for you?''

She fumbled for her planner. "What time?"

"You choose."

How about never? "Noon?"

"Fine."

Silence spun out.

Then they both spoke at once.

"Dev, I don't think—"

"If you need to call—" He paused, like her
words had just registered. "Look, this doesn't have
to be painful. A simple picnic, that's all. For a good
cause."

It will be painful. It can't be anything else. But
she was too much Margaret DeMille's daughter to
say so, and the cause was important. One hand
pressing against her stomach, Lacey spoke again.
"I have a three o'clock tennis match at the club.
That shouldn't be a problem, do you think?" There.
She'd put a time limit on it. Two hours, max.

How would she ever get through two hours alone
with Dev?

A wry chuckle sounded in her ear. "Tell you
what. I'll just give you my voice mail number so
it's easier for you to cancel."

"I won't cancel."

"I won't hold my breath." He gave her a phone
number with a Dallas area code. "But I'd appreciate it if you'd cancel by Friday so I don't have to
make the drive."

"I won't cancel, Dev."

He paused before he answered. "Then you'll surprise me."

His tone turned impersonal again. "I'll call you when I get to town, and we'll work out logistics." Then he hung up without even saying goodbye.

"I won't cancel, Dev," she whispered once more, into a silent phone.

She wouldn't. But oh, how she wished she could.

Chapter Three

Dev knocked on the door of the frame house that his mother had lived in for twelve years.

Muffled by the door, a voice called out, "Come on in."

He turned the knob and stepped inside, bracing in reflex. Waiting...always expecting his mother's four-month sobriety to have come to an end.

But the scent of coffee, not liquor, greeted him on this Saturday morning after his return from Houston.

Coffee...and the sight of his mother sitting on the living room floor surrounded by boxes, holding a tie in her hands, a wistful smile on her face.

Monique Marlowe looked up. "Do you remember this tie? Your father called it his lucky tie. Wore

it whenever he had to deal with the IRS or a difficult client.'' She held it out to him.

Dev stepped over boxes and squatted down beside her, worried at the moisture glistening on her
lashes. "You could leave this stuff to us, Mom.
We'll go through it.''

Her once-black hair had gone snow-white suddenly, as if her battle with the bottle had drained
everything from her. "No, Devlin. These are my
memories. It's taken me almost twenty years to face
them. I need to deal with them myself.'' She
stroked one finger down the tie, an unremarkable
regimental in shades of navy and burgundy.

And suddenly, Dev did remember it, knotted
around Patrick Marlowe's neck. For one instant, he
could feel his father's hand clap his shoulder, could
see the green eyes he'd inherited sparkling with
pride as his father spoke. *"Will you look at this boy,
Monique? He'll be as tall as me soon. Our Dev is
growing up."*

Dev had probably been twelve, three years away
from the worst day of his life.

At least, the worst day until he and Lacey—

"Would you like to have the tie, Devlin?''

"No.'' He saw the hurt in her eyes at his curt
tone. He shook his head and exhaled. "I'm sorry.
I drove in from Houston, got here just before
seven.'' And still couldn't get any damn sleep.
"You have any coffee made, Mom? Then I'll give
you a hand here.''

His mother held out a hand for assistance, and
Dev tugged her to her feet, the grace she'd never
lost, even at her worst, doing most of the work.

Monique Marlowe had been a lovely drunk. She'd never turned slovenly, had coped—in her own way. If she couldn't handle four children or the realities of a life of poverty, still she'd held on to the one thing that had always been hers—her beauty. At sixty-two, she bore some of the lines of age but she was still too beautiful to be a grandmother.

But thank God she was. Dierdre's child had been the surprising magic that had transformed her. Had given her what her children could not—a reason to stay sober.

"Poor Devlin," she murmured, reaching up to stroke his cheek. "You work too hard." The lovely blue eyes turned uncertain, and she looked down at her hands. "All this has made me think about a lot of things. I—I've never apologized to you, son. It wasn't right what I did when Patrick—" Her eyelashes batted rapidly, but a single tear spilled over.

Dev clasped her slender shoulders. "Don't, Mom. It's over. You're doing well, and that's all that matters." What was done was done...and his own emotions were stretched too thin to have this discussion after last night.

After Lacey.

He wasn't ready to rehash the past. Not now. Not when he still carried the feel of Lacey's slim hand in his, when those silvery eyes wouldn't let him sleep.

"I still don't understand it. The Patrick I knew was no crook. He was so angry, so hurt, so—" She looked up at her son, blue eyes swimming with pain. "It literally killed him, the disgrace."

"He had a weak heart, Mom. He was under a lot of stress." With the Securities and Exchange Commission findings of fraud, his father's whole career had been on the line. Even if he'd escaped conviction, he'd never have worked in a high-powered accounting firm like DeMille and Marshall again.

She gripped his sleeve. "But do you believe he did it?"

Dev was too tired for this discussion. Too many years had passed, and he'd been too young. All he'd known was that his father was dead, that with shocking suddenness, their expansive lifestyle had crashed around them. No more soccer games. No more vacations. Only the grim struggle to survive.

Only the shame.

But his mother's gaze still pinned him, waiting for a response.

"I don't know what to think. All I cared about back then was getting my driver's license." He'd forgotten that—how driving had seemed all-important at fifteen.

He patted her hand. "It doesn't matter, Mom. None of it matters now. We go forward, isn't that what they tell you in your meetings? You're doing great. Don't let the past snare you in its trap."

Remember that, Dev. The past is the past.

His mother's eyes swirled with confusion, with old hurts. With the beginnings of the fog that had claimed too many years.

Dev swore silently at the sight. "Come on, Mom. You've worked too hard to get here." He gestured at the boxes. "I'll get Connor and Dee to help me, and we'll get rid of this stuff."

Visibly, she pulled herself back, the new woman she was becoming. Drawing in a deep breath, she shook her head. "No, Devlin. These are my memories. I haven't been able to look at any of this since he—" Again, she shook her head. "There's one box of your father's business papers that I'd like you to take, though. I don't understand any of that stuff, but I thought you might like to have them."

The last thing he wanted was to dig into their past. His own past with Lacey was plenty to handle right now. But he nodded. "I'll stick it in my car when I leave. I'm pretty busy on a case right now, but I'll get to it one of these days. Or maybe I'll take it to Connor. Let him put that MBA to use for something besides impressing women."

Monique smiled faintly at the thought of Dev's much younger brother. "You're a good son, Devlin. A good man. I've let you down, but I won't do that anymore." She lifted her shoulders, straightening her whole delicate frame. "Once I move, I'm going to look for a job. You've supported me long enough. Too long."

"You have an important job, Mom. Grandmother. Little Katie is going to keep you plenty busy." Seeing her protest, he shook his head. "Don't worry about it right now, okay? I'm doing fine." Then, unable to stand any more assaults from the past, he took the tie from her hand and laid it on the sofa, then steered her toward the kitchen. "But if you wanted to fix me breakfast while I drink about a gallon of coffee, I sure wouldn't complain."

"I'd be happy to do that."

"Good. And while you're at it, you can tell me what the world's smartest baby has been up to this week."

At the mention of Dierdre's Katie, his mother's eyes lit. "Oh, that sweet child. You won't believe what she did just yesterday...."

He could tell this would take a while, but that was fine. Dev would forgive Dierdre all the attempts at matchmaking that drove him nuts. She'd produced the miracle that had given his mother a reason to live.

And listening to stories of sweet Katie was far better than thinking about whether or not Lacey would cancel their picnic.

And whether or not he hoped she would.

Lacey held Christina's hand as they entered the plastic surgeon's office. The surgeon was an associate of Philip's who'd agreed to give an assessment on reconstructing the child's face.

Christina clasped her hand tightly, her head downcast. The child had learned too much about the world's cruelty. The stares bothered her, whether from pity or disgust. The pretty pink dress Lacey had bought her to wear today, knowing how much Christina minded being seen in public, wasn't helping, no matter Christina's delight when she'd donned it.

"Let's sit over here, all right?" Lacey's hand hovered over the fine strawberry-blond hair and she resisted the urge to warn the room's other occupants to be careful of this child.

But instead, she found her own heart tugged. A

boy of perhaps twelve sat with his mother, his hands and face bearing the scars of terrible burns. The boy glanced up, then away quickly, as she'd seen Christina do so often. Lacey wished she could tell the boy he had nothing to fear from her, but the best she could do was to meet the mother's gaze evenly, with a nod and a smile. The woman glanced at Christina and smiled back.

"Lacey." Christina tugged her down and whispered in Lacey's ear. "That boy—he's got scars, too." Her brown eyes were filled with sympathy. "Did someone hit him?"

Dear God, it was so unfair that an eight-year-old girl should have lived the way Christina had. Lacey leaned down. "If we whisper about him, he'll feel like you feel when people stare. Could we talk about this later?"

Understanding dawned. Christina nodded. Looking across the room, she gave the boy a shy smile. It wasn't returned, but the boy didn't turn away quite so far this time.

"Let's read a magazine," Lacey suggested, rising to head for the magazine rack.

Just then, the door to the examining rooms opened, and Missy Delavant stepped out. She looked startled to see Lacey, but somehow Lacey couldn't be too surprised that this woman who hadn't yet hit thirty would already be looking into cosmetic surgery.

"Lacey, what are you doing here?" Missy's mouth took on a sly smirk.

"I'm here with a client."

"Client?" Missy glanced behind Lacey. It was

easy to tell when she spotted Christina from the look of distaste that crossed her face. "Oh—one of your little urchins, right? Philip told me about your volunteer work. I have to hand it to you, Lacey—I don't know how you do it. Philip's idea of serving on the hospital board sounds much less…tawdry."

Years under Margaret DeMille's tutelage kept the sharp retort from Lacey's lips, but her hands curled at her sides. "I enjoy my work. It's very satisfying."

But Missy wasn't through sharpening her claws. "As satisfying as selling your picnic for five thousand dollars? I thought your mother would choke." Her eyebrows lifted. "But the hunk who bought it…" She licked her lips.

The last thing Lacey wanted to discuss was Dev. "I'd better get back to Christina."

Missy still had one more parting shot. "You should be careful, Lacey. Philip is more than a little miffed about this little pas de deux picnic. He says you've been making yourself scarce the last few days. Is there something going on with the dream boat? Doesn't look too good for Philip's fiancée to be dating another man."

"It's not a date. And Philip and I are not engaged."

Missy's eyes widened. "But it's only a matter of time, isn't it? Or is there more you're not telling?"

Only that I can't sleep and I've picked up the phone a hundred times to cancel—

"It's a simple fund-raiser, Missy. End of story. Now if you'll excuse me, Christina's nervous about being here and I need to be with her.'' Lacey turned away.

''Nice to see you, Lacey. Let me know if you need a substitute for the picnic.''

If only it were that simple.

Lacey sat down by Christina. ''Here—this one looks interesting. Why don't you read this story to me?''

When she heard the door close, Lacey let out the breath she'd been holding.

Dev sipped his coffee as he looked out at the Houston morning, then glanced at his watch again. The princess might not be a morning person, but she'd been gone when he'd gotten into Houston late last night and tried to call. He'd have to call her soon.

He could have simply left a message on her answering machine with the time he'd pick her up, but he wanted to hear it from her own voice. She might say she wouldn't cancel, but he wouldn't put it past her. Wouldn't be the first time she had left him hanging.

He looked at his watch again. Nine o'clock. Accustomed to rising at five to work out at the gym, he felt as if it was noon. It would be impolite to wait any longer to call, even if he woke her up.

On the fourth ring, the answering machine picked up. Dev listened to the voice that had haunted his dreams until he had ruthlessly quashed them in the struggle to survive.

Lacey's voice had been clear and pure back then, the melodic tones of a bell. Now it held an undertone that made Dev think of the smooth wood-smoked whiskey he favored. Just a little edge of sex beneath the patrician.

Once he had felt the first licks of flame beneath the girl's innocence. Had the woman learned to burn or had she frozen solid?

He was surprised at how much he wanted to know.

Just as the recorded message was ending, he heard the real voice break in—and felt it like a caress across raw nerves.

"Hello?" Just a hint of smoke and velvet beneath cool satin.

His body stirred, and Dev wanted to hang up.

"Hello?" Irritation edged at sleep.

"Sleeping late again, princess?"

"I didn't—" He heard her suck in a gasp. "Oh, no—" Her voice took on a note of horror. "Dev, it's nine o'clock—"

"I noticed." He sat down on the bed, enjoying the sense of advantage. "Not much of an early riser, are you? I guess that's easy when you don't have to work for a living."

"Dev, I don't usually—"

He could almost feel ashamed at the distress he heard. This wasn't much of a way to get their picnic started, and it sure as hell was no way to pave the path for Boone and Maddie.

"It doesn't matter." He tamped down his irritation, running fingers through his hair. "I owe you an apology. I got out of Dallas too late last night and you weren't home when I called. I'm sorry if I'm calling too early."

"It's not too early," she responded. "I'm not a late sleeper. I just—"

"Does this give you enough time to get ready?"

"Three hours? I could be ready in thirty minutes." She sniffed.

"No woman can get ready in thirty minutes. I know. I have sisters."

Then she surprised him. "Want to bet?"

"I beg your pardon?"

"Would you care to make a wager, Mr. Marlowe?"

Damn, but he could almost get a kick out of that snotty princess-to-peasant tone. Except that he was tired of being the peasant. But this Lacey intrigued him. He decided to push her further.

"Are we talking thirty minutes from the time I hang up the phone?"

"I—"

He heard the note of panic in her voice. "Shall we synchronize our watches?"

"Dev, I— Maybe I was a little hasty."

"Ah. I knew it. My sisters always had to change clothes fourteen times. And then there's all that makeup and the hair and junk. Don't worry, I understand."

He should pull the receiver away from his ear before he got frostbite. He could feel ice forming now.

"Fine. Thirty minutes from the time we hang up. But that will make our picnic rather early."

"Hey, nine o'clock is like noon to me. Some of us working stiffs have to get up early."

Ice turned to steel, encased in velvet. "So how much shall we wager?"

The challenge was irresistible. And damn it, he was surprised by this Lacey. Maybe the doe wasn't so fragile after all.

"Not how much. When."

"What do you mean?"

"If you lose, we have a real date."

He heard a faint gasp, but she recovered quickly. "And if I win?"

Dev smiled. "Then you get to pick where we go."

Lacey laughed, and it felt like the first warm spring shower washing over a heart chilled by winter. "You always dared too much, Dev. Always pushed the limits."

Yeah. And lost big, thanks to your father.

The past rose up between them, and the warmth of the moment slid away. Dev was surprised that he wasn't ready to let it go. "So does that mean you agree?"

Silence sang out over the line.

"Dev, do you think this is wise?"

The girl who had dared to meet him in defiance of her father warred with the princess who knew her place.

And his.

"Probably not. Your father wouldn't like it at all."

"My father has nothing to do with this."

Keep telling yourself that, princess. "Forget the bet. I'll pick you up at noon." He prepared to hang up.

Frost coated a clear challenge. ''I'll be ready in thirty minutes, Dev.''

He shook his head, not sure whether to marvel or curse. She wasn't a shy sixteen-year-old anymore.

''Okay. You're on.''

Lacey threw the third change of clothes on her bed. What did one wear to a picnic with a man who'd betrayed her? She fumbled in her purse for the roll of antacids.

Why had she agreed to this? What was she thinking, to have let him manipulate her into this picnic—much less to bet with him, for heavens' sake? She never lost her temper, but somehow he had pushed her too far with that smug certainty, with all his assumptions.

She stood for a moment, hands on hips, and reached for her usual aplomb. Casual, Lacey. Pick something casual so he'll know you don't care.

Did she own anything casual? She reached for her Donna Karan wraparound skirt and a simple gray silk T-shirt.

The phone rang.

Glancing at the clock, Lacey touched her stomach. She yanked both garments off their hangers and walked to the phone. ''Hello?''

''Lacey, darling. How are you today?''

Oh, no. ''I'm fine, Mother. How are you?'' Lacey pulled on her panty hose, then stripped them right off. Sandals. She'd wear sandals. Sandals were casual.

''You sound out of breath.''

"Oh, I'm just—" Out of her mind, that's what she was. Insane to have agreed to this picnic. "I'm exercising, Mother. May I call you back?"

"Why…yes." The voice went frosty. "I suppose that will be all right. How much longer do you have left? I must leave in forty-five minutes for bridge."

"Oh, dear. I'll probably miss you, then. I just now got started. What did you need?" *Please hurry, Mother.* Lacey pulled the phone away from her ear as she slipped on her top. "What?"

"I said, are you all right? You sound distracted."

"Fine…just fine. I, um—I'm warmed up and didn't want to let my muscles cool." Lacey frowned at herself in the mirror. The color wasn't right. Casting a frantic glance at her closet, she was headed across the floor when the doorbell rang.

"Is that your doorbell?"

"No—uh, yes. I guess it is. Listen, Mother, I'll talk to you later, all right?"

"Go answer it and I'll wait. I need to talk to you about this picnic. Darling, it's simply not suitable. You know nothing about this man."

The doorbell rang again, twice this time. *No woman can be ready in thirty minutes.*

"Mother, I'm sorry. I'll have to talk to you later. Have a good time at bridge." Knowing she would pay for it later, Lacey hung up the phone and grabbed her skirt, fastening it around her waist as she ran to the closet and slid her feet into high-heeled, strappy sandals.

Casting a glance at the mirror, she frowned. No lipstick. Hair barely dry.

He was knocking this time. Lacey made a face at herself in the mirror and headed for the door.

The door burst open, and there she was, color high in her cheeks and breathing hard.

She was gorgeous.

And rattled.

For a moment the past fled, and he couldn't resist teasing. "Sure you're ready?"

There it went, that regal lift of the chin. "I told you I'd be ready," Lacey replied tartly. "I'll get my things." She turned and walked with unhurried grace down the hallway. Her shirttail was untucked in the back.

Dev grinned. Then he closed the door behind him and looked around. What he saw surprised him.

Mostly he saw the *Architectural Digest* spread he'd expected. A lot of whites and creams, high windows and open spaces. It could have been sterile, except that here and there were bold splashes of color. Reds and purples and golds in fat pillows and lush paintings hinting at the passion he'd found inside the ethereal virgin princess.

He wanted to see more, to prowl her bedroom, to find out if the passion still lived inside the woman she'd become.

But it didn't matter. This was business. Passion hadn't kept her from betraying him.

She returned with the picnic basket and a quilt, a tiny excuse for a purse dangling from her shoulder, lipstick applied and shirt tucked inside the narrow waist. Her legs seemed to go on forever.

He took the basket from her. "You didn't need the lipstick. You look fine without it."

The princess started, then quickly recovered. But her eyes, those silvery, witchy eyes, studied him for a long breath. One hand grazed her stomach lightly.

A surge of something like guilt assaulted Dev's conscience. He'd seen her touch her stomach like that before.

"Do you feel all right?"

She looked startled. "Yes, of course. Why do you ask?"

Dev nodded at her hand, and she dropped it to her side as if burned.

"I'm perfectly fine." Frost crackled in her tone. "Shall we go?"

He studied her carefully, seeing the line between her brows, the slight pinch to her face. He'd learn nothing if he alienated her. *Keep it light, Dev. Keep it light.*

"Your chariot awaits, milady." Only a trace of sarcasm escaped as Dev reached for the doorknob. "After you."

Lacey skirted the door frame as she preceded him. He was so…physical. Too physical. The boy had been more than she'd known how to handle. The man…

Dream boat, Missy had called him. She wasn't wrong. Not classically handsome, Dev was undeniably magnetic. In a tux, he'd been striking, but she wasn't sure that she didn't prefer him in today's more casual attire, jeans and a short-sleeved khaki shirt. His raven's-wing black hair was cut short, but one lock of it was as rebellious as the boy she'd once known, tumbling down on his forehead in a way that made her fingers itch to touch it.

He took money and walked away, Lacey. She had to remember that he'd been great to look at back then, too.

That crooked smile and the once-broken nose only added character to a face that was far too attractive to her. Clever mind, brilliant green eyes that looked too closely, a sense that when he was listening to you, nothing else interfered with his concentration. It felt like being caught in the glow of a brilliant floodlamp, with nowhere to hide.

A lady does not seek the limelight, Lacey. In her mother's world, a lady only attracted public attention three times in her life—at birth, when she married and when she died.

"Over here," Dev directed, his hand settling lightly against her waist.

The heat of his hand distracted her until they were almost upon his car. She stopped in her tracks. "This is yours?"

Green eyes turned to glass. "It'll get us where we're going. If you're lucky, none of your friends will see us in it."

"That's not what I—" But it was too late. He'd shut her door and rounded the back to place the basket in the trunk.

Just great, Lacey. Offend him before you even make it to the park.

Two hours. It might as well be eons.

Chapter Four

Hermann Park spread out before them in all its lush green glory. Lacey had chosen it over the grounds of the Menil Museum she'd originally planned to use for her auction contribution. She wanted lots of people around them. Intimacy with Devlin Marlowe was to be avoided at all costs.

The day was sunny and humid, but fall had at last decided to visit Houston. Temperatures had finally dropped into the seventies, thank goodness.

Dev parked the car. "This all right?"

She looked straight ahead and only nodded.

He muttered something under his breath and jerked his door handle open. The heavy door slammed behind him.

Lacey reached for her own door handle, feeling a shiver run through her. She couldn't do this.

I'll take care of it. Her father's words echoed in her head.

It's only a picnic, Daddy, she had said. *I can handle it.*

But she'd never handled Devlin Marlowe. She'd been too mesmerized by him, been putty in his hands.

He used you, Lacey. He didn't love you. That was your foolish dream, she thought. If her father hadn't shown up that night, he'd have taken her virginity and he still would have left.

And now he was back to rub it in. To show her how successful he was, that he wasn't her father's gofer anymore. She'd never thought of Dev as cruel, but then she'd been so sick in love with him that she'd never dreamed he'd trade her for money, either. She'd begged him, for heaven's sake. Begged him to be the first. Cherished all the dreams he'd whispered in the night, thought that love was all that was important.

She'd been so naive. Such a romantic. But she wasn't sixteen anymore.

Anger began to steady her. Lacey seldom allowed herself the luxury of anger, but right now she welcomed its heat, its ability to scorch away the scar tissue, reopen the wound of how badly Dev had hurt her.

I'll show him that it didn't matter. That I don't care.

And she thanked her mother for all the lessons on presenting a serene face to people she couldn't abide.

Carefully, Lacey drew her own face into that

mask. When her door flew open, she flinched but recovered quickly. With studied grace, she alighted from the car, her gaze skipping right past Dev's.

"Would you like me to carry the quilt?" she asked.

Dev heard the polite tone, saw the elegant disdain. With great effort, he forced back the rage that swamped him.

So they were back to that. Princess to peasant.

Fine. Two could play this game. She thought he was a barbarian not fit to clean her dainty slippers. He would show her that the years had taken off the rough edges.

"I've got it," he said evenly. "You pick the spot."

She looked everywhere but at him, finally nodding toward a huge live oak spreading its deep shade on a slight rise about a hundred yards away.

"After you, princess." For a moment, he thought he saw her flinch from his tone and knew he'd have to work harder to cover how much she unsettled him.

He'd faced enraged husbands he'd caught cheating, boxing opponents out to tear off his head, vicious drunken fellow GIs out to prove who was more man. None of them had rattled him like this delicate creature crossing the grass on legs that could stop traffic.

That was the other challenge. Even if he could bury the sense of betrayal deeply enough to keep his head, what did he do about the hunger of his body for hers? It was as if all the years in between had never existed…only this time it was much worse. She wasn't a young girl he needed to treat with kid gloves. She might be delicately made, but she was a full-grown woman who made his body burn. He wanted to get his hands on her worse than he wanted his next breath, and knowing how she'd betrayed him didn't seem to mean a damn to the ache in his gut.

How could he want her worse than ever, after all this time? After what he knew she was, how he knew she saw him?

Dev's temper was barely in check by the time they reached the tree. Holding his jaw so tight he thought he'd crack a tooth, he set down the basket and busied himself spreading the quilt, refusing to look at her while he cursed the part of him that was ruling his brain.

Lacey knelt on the quilt, folding those tempting legs beneath her, and opened the basket, still not looking at him.

It made him madder than hell.

Boone and Maddie and Mitch, he thought, chanting the names silently like a mantra. *They're your friends. Don't blow this.*

But he didn't know what to say to her, how to move his thoughts up to that superficial level.

He might have known she would. Her tone careful, she spoke while gracefully setting out plates and silverware rolled in heavy, expensive napkins. "So what do you do for a living, Dev?"

I find out secrets. Like yours. "I'm a private investigator."

Her head lifted quickly, the surprise smoothing

over so quickly he might have imagined it. "Like Sam Spade?"

Clever. She had a sense of humor.

"Yeah. Left my fedora at home, though. Hope it doesn't ruin the image."

Lacey laughed, and it flowed over his hearing like water in the desert, light and fresh and too delicious for his own good.

But it helped. It pulled him back from the anger.

She looked at him then, the silvery eyes bright. For just a second, he thought he saw regret slip across them like a shadow over the sun.

"I don't mind. You don't have the accent, though. You'd need to be more gruff."

He pitched his voice to a growl. "You dames are all alike. A guy's tough, you want him gentle like some damn poet. He's a soft touch, you want him dangerous."

Lacey's hands stilled on the crackers she was carefully arranging around a half-wheel of Brie.

Memory and desire scorched the air around them.

Dangerous, Lacey thought. Then and now. She'd loved his edge, loved the way he made her feel so alive. As though wild was something she could be, too. He'd swept into her life like a hurricane, like a dragon breathing fire and danger. He'd broken into her safe little world like a cat burglar, and she'd reveled in the delicious thrill.

Then like a good cat burglar, before she'd realized it, he'd stolen her heart and every last shred of her common sense. She'd taken risks with him that she'd never dreamed of before—or since.

She was careful now. Always so careful.

She busied herself again with the crackers, setting the plate closer to him. She forced her voice back to lightness. "So who do you work for?"

"No one." His voice was hard. "I'll never take orders from anyone again."

It wouldn't serve to dig deeper. Light was what they needed now. "So do you do things like sneak around in the dark and catch cheating husbands?"

"Not if I can help it." The edge sharpened.

She hadn't asked it right. "I'm sorry. I phrased that poorly. I wasn't being snide. I only know what I read or see in the movies." She forced her gaze up to him, her apology sincere. "What exactly does a private investigator do?"

His frame relaxed. Leaning back on one hand, he propped the other arm on his upraised knee. "Lots of them do exactly that. Divorce cases are a staple. Or working for lawyers, digging up background information for trials."

"But not you?"

Dev shrugged. "I've done my share, but most of what my agency does is corporate background checks."

"Other people work for you?"

He nodded, and she thought she saw the gleam of pride. "I went to work for the former owner parttime after I got out of the service, then wound up buying the business when he wanted to retire. It was small potatoes then, but I've got ten investigators working for me now."

"Do you still investigate, too?"

A strange look crossed his face so quickly she

might have imagined it. He nodded. "I've gained a reputation for being able to find people."

"What kind of people?"

"Missing. Any kind. Vanished spouses, missing children—" He straightened abruptly, scanning the offerings. "So what do we have here?"

Lacey took the hint and didn't press. It didn't matter anyway—she wouldn't see him again after today. "It's only marginally healthy, but I hope you like it. Foie gras, Brie, water biscuits, fruit—" She reached into the basket and pulled out a bottle. "Chardonnay—would you like to check the vintage?"

Dev glanced up to see if she was testing him, but she seemed sincere. Torn between demonstrating that he did understand wines now and knowing that it shouldn't matter, he merely shrugged. "I'll trust your judgment. Want me to open it?"

She smiled. "Please." Picking up a plate, she began to select food for him. "Tell me if there's something here you don't like."

I don't like having to be here and play nicey-nice with you, Lacey. I don't like having to pretend I don't want to touch you. Taste you.

But he didn't say that. He clamped down hard on the hunger and instead turned the tables, though he wasn't sure she could tell him much that he didn't already know.

"So who's the overgrown frat boy?"

Her head jerked up. "What?"

"The blond pretty boy with you at the auction. He your boyfriend?"

"He's…" She glanced away. "We date. He's a doctor, a plastic surgeon named Philip Forrester."

Dev laughed without mirth. "Well, if you marry him that should come in handy when you reach the right age."

Her frame tensed, her eyes sparking, but her voice was smooth as glass. "I suppose you're referring to a face-lift, but I don't plan to ever do that."

"You'll be drummed out of River Oaks, you know." He softened the earlier insult with a teasing tone. "I think it's in the deed restrictions."

Her mouth quirked. "I saw an acquaintance when I took Christina to another plastic surgeon the other day. This woman is only twenty-nine, and she's already making plans."

Dev snorted. "That's pathetic. Wrinkles show you've lived. Lines of character don't make a woman ugly."

Lacey's eyes softened. "You really believe that?"

"You've lived in the glass bubble too long. In the real world, appearances aren't everything, Lacey."

To his surprise, she didn't get offended. She merely shook her head sadly. "Sometimes they matter too much, even in the real world."

Dev frowned. "Why do you say that?" He thought back to her earlier words. "Who's Christina?"

Her whole face changed. He saw affection there, and sorrow.

"She's an eight-year-old girl for whom I'm an advocate."

"What kind of advocate?" He thought back to a family court case he'd worked. "You mean a child advocate for abused kids?"

Lacey nodded. "It's one of the projects of the Junior League. Volunteers represent the abused or neglected child's best interest, monitoring them in either substitute care or foster care, coordinating with the caseworker, doing the background work to help the judge decide the best place for the child to wind up."

Dev looked at her through new eyes. This wasn't playing Lady Bountiful and donating canned goods at Christmas. "So why did you have Christina at the plastic surgeon's?"

Anger warred with sorrow on her lovely face. "One of her mother's boyfriends beat her badly when she was four. He broke bones in her face and she didn't get proper care. The bones healed wrong, and her face is distorted. She's been taken away from her mother and is in foster care, but once she's available for adoption, her condition will greatly reduce her chances because the surgery she needs is very expensive."

Her gaze lifted to his, pain stark in those lovely eyes. "Other children make fun of her, and she gets stared at on the street." Her look was almost pleading, her hands gripping one another so tightly her knuckles were white. "She's the sweetest child, and it's so unfair. If only people could see past—" Her voice broke.

"So you're going to get her the surgery." It

wasn't a question, and once again, Dev frowned. She didn't sound like the princess.

Her shoulders sank. "I want to, but it's complicated by her legal position." Then she squared her shoulders and lifted her chin. "But I've gotten the assessment that I needed. We're not supposed to get personally involved, but what she needs can be done, and I'm going to find a way to make it happen."

"So what do your parents think about this?"

Her mouth pursed. "It doesn't matter."

I doubt that. But he wanted to cheer for the signs of a Lacey who might not be so docile.

"And the fiancé?"

She drew right inside her Margaret DeMille shell. "We're not engaged."

"Everyone else seems to think you are."

"*What* everyone else?" Suddenly, the glass-calm surface rippled. Her eyes narrowed. "I thought you didn't know—have you been investigating me, Devlin Marlowe?"

He'd always been one hell of a poker player. Sometimes half the truth would work. Lazily, he lifted an eyebrow. "I asked a few questions at the auction. The consensus seems to be that you'll be Mrs. Doctor before long."

"Who said that?"

"A woman who obviously hopes she's wrong. I think she's got her eye on your doctor."

"He's not my doctor," she snapped. "My parents—"

"Your parents like him, right? Daddy approves? Dr. Blondie is just about good enough for his princess?'' Dev shrugged elaborately, clamping down on the burn in his gut. ''It's a perfect fit. Society princess marries rich doctor. They have two point two children and live happily ever after in River Oaks.'' It was cruel but it was true, and it enraged him. ''That's what you were raised to be, Lacey. So what's your beef?''

For a moment they sat there like warring opponents, her slender frame singing with tension, his jaw tight.

Then Dev couldn't stand it anymore. Memories clashed, and he was back in a moon-silvered gazebo being told he wasn't good enough to touch the princess. The princess who'd turned away when he'd laid his heart at her feet.

''Go to hell, Devlin.'' Her voice shook, but her eyes spit fire.

He grabbed her by the arms and hauled her against his body. ''I've been there,'' he muttered. Then he covered her mouth with his.

And for an instant, that twice-damned mouth yielded to his hunger. For just a breath, he felt her respond as if all the years between had meant nothing. He'd expected resistance, anticipated ice.

Instead he got fire, and it scorched through his blood.

Gut-deep desire vaporized thought. His body responded so fast, his head spun. Caught between the past and the present, his only thought was to get closer—

She jerked her mouth away and slapped him. Hard. Then she leaped to her feet.

''Don't you ever touch me again.'' Her voice

was thready. Slivers of ice rose in her devastated gaze.

Dev jumped to his feet to pull her back, to—

To what? What the hell was he doing?

Lacey bent and retrieved her purse, then shot him a glare that should have sliced him to the bone. "I'll—" Her voice shook, just slightly, then he watched as her mother's training took control.

In a voice that could have frozen a blast furnace, she spoke. "I'll call a cab. I think you got your money's worth, and if you didn't, I don't care." She turned to walk away.

"Lacey, wait—" When she didn't, he slid a hand through his hair and clasped the back of his neck, afraid to touch her again. "I'll drive you home."

She kept walking, so he took off after her.

"If you touch me again, I'll call the police."

He could see she meant it. He wanted to blast her with angry words, wanted to have it all out right here. Right now.

But then he looked at her again and saw the one thing he couldn't fight.

She was shaking. She was afraid of him, no matter what she said.

And that hit him where it hurt.

"Look, I'm sorry. I had no right to do that."

But she was already hitting speed dial on her cell phone. "I'd like a cab right away. Hermann Park near the Museum of Fine Arts." She listened for a moment. "Five minutes will be fine." She punched it off.

"Lacey, I said I'm sorry."

She stared straight ahead. "It doesn't matter."

Looking at her utterly blank expression, he could almost believe that was true.

"Call the cab off. I'll drive you home. I won't touch you."

He saw her slender shoulders sag just slightly, then straighten. "I don't need the basket anymore. Enjoy your meal, Dev. I hope it was everything you wanted."

She turned toward him, just slightly, and the nerves in her eyes stopped him cold.

Good God. If he had set out to screw everything up, he couldn't have done any better.

He had to think what to do, had to readjust his plan. Had to—

"There's a cab. Goodbye, Dev." With the grace that was her trademark, she walked away across the grass without ever looking back.

Dev watched her go, feeling edgy and ragged with the debris of desire. Feeling like the lowest form of scum.

He'd started out to prove that he'd become civilized over the years. He thought he had. Would have sworn it.

Apparently not. Something about Lacey still spoke to him at a level far deeper than any acquired polish.

Score two points for the bad boy who'd just revealed his true colors.

Back to square one.

Chapter Five

Lacey stepped inside her front door and slipped off her shoes, padding across the entry in stocking feet as she flipped through her mail. It was Friday afternoon, and she'd been wrangling with bureaucrats all day over Christina. She was hardly in the mood to attend her parents' cocktail party tonight, but not going was out of the question.

She dropped the entire stack of mail on the entry table, not caring what was in it. Maybe if she'd had a decent night's sleep all week, things would be different.

But she hadn't. Every time she closed her eyes, Dev was there, lying in wait. She could stay busy during her waking hours, busy enough to shove him away, to forget the fiasco of that picnic.

Of that kiss.

But at night...alone in the darkness, he leaped every barrier. Night had been their time. Under cover of darkness, Dev had shown her a world light-years away from her own. He'd shown her passion...and freedom...and made her question, tempted her to follow him away from the safe life she'd known.

Then he'd abandoned her. Never bothered to see if she was all right after the night she'd flown high in his arms—

And then crashed to earth.

So why, the one time she was back in those strong arms, had she yielded, even for one second? Why had he felt so treacherously right?

Lacey eyed the deep cushions of her sofa. She glanced in the mirror and didn't like what she saw. Maybe a quick nap would help smooth out the rough edges. Her mother had eyes like heat-seeking missiles. Lacey needed to be sharp and on her toes.

She crossed the room and sank into the sofa's embrace. *It's daylight, Dev. You have to leave me alone.*

In seconds, she slid under, tired to the bone.

It seemed like only seconds later when she struggled to the surface, frowning as she tried to shake the cobwebs and figure out what had pulled her back.

The door. Someone was knocking.

Lacey closed her eyes. Go away, she thought.

But whoever it was didn't give up. Staggering slightly, she made it from the sofa to the door, glancing through the glass and going stiff with shock.

No.

Lacey shook her head and squeezed her eyes. She was still dreaming, surely.

But she opened them again, and there he was.

Lacey drew a deep breath and pressed one hand to her stomach as she struggled for the mask she needed. She opened the door.

"Hello, Dev." She tried to put in her tone all the detachment she wanted to feel.

From behind his back, he pulled out her basket, his tone light but his green eyes giving more away. "I brought back your basket."

"I told you I didn't need it." *Go away, Dev.* He was devastating in a black T-shirt and black slacks. The T-shirt clung to a very well-developed chest she could still feel against her body.

"I know." With his free hand, he brushed at the errant lock that had always plagued him, his fingers raking through his raven hair. "I probably should have just shipped it back to you, but—"

Emerald eyes pinned hers. "I owe you an apology. I needed to deliver it in person."

Lacey's hand went slack on the door handle. She felt like ten miles of bad road and probably looked worse. She needed all her defenses to handle Dev, and sleep still fogged her brain. "I—Dev, it's been a long week. I don't—"

"Please, Lacey." On his too-interesting face, she read real regret. "Let me talk to you for just a minute."

She glanced down at her wrinkled linen suit, her unshod feet. "Can you give me a minute? I—I'm afraid I fell asleep. I must look dreadful—" She stepped away from the door and gestured him inside.

His piercing eyes studied her. His voice was slightly husky as he spoke. "You look beautiful, as always." Then his gaze softened, his voice dropping low. "Are you all right?"

She realized she had one hand pressed against her abdomen. Like she'd touched a hot burner, she jerked it away. "I'm perfectly fine. Just let me—" Turning away, she spoke over her shoulder. "Have a seat. I'll be right back."

Crossing her bedroom, she shed her suit jacket, then headed for the bathroom and carefully splashed cold water on her face. Patting it dry, she stared at herself in the mirror, taking in the dark shadows beneath her eyes. She applied new lipstick and spritzed on perfume, then cursed herself for caring how she looked.

Good grooming is a woman's best armor, darling. Margaret DeMille would sooner be drawn and quartered than appear before the eyes of another human without impeccable makeup and perfectly coifed hair.

The way Lacey looked, Dev would be out there for hours if she were to meet her mother's goal. Turning away from the mirror with a sigh, she headed back to the living room, detouring by the entry table to slip on her heels.

Reaching for composure, she drew in a deep breath, then headed for Dev. "Would you care for something to drink?" She stopped with the coffee table securely between them.

"No, I—" He stopped abruptly, studying her closely, then exhaled. "All right. Sure."

He was nervous, Lacey marveled. Seeing it steadied her. "Iced tea, or something stronger?" Wondering at herself for the urge, she gave in and teased. "I might be able to find a good Chardonnay."

He'd been glancing around the room, but his head whipped toward her, his look intense. When he saw the curve of her lips, for a fleeting instant his lips answered, his smile wry. "I'd better stay away from Chardonnay. Seems to make me do stupid things." His chest rose. "Lacey, I—"

She wasn't ready. "Iced tea it is, then." She headed for the kitchen, willing strength into legs that had gone weak with the force of that crooked smile.

But he followed her. As she put ice in glasses, he stood in the center of her kitchen looking too good. Hands thrust in his pockets, he scanned the room. "Can I help?"

She shook her head and concentrated on the glasses.

"Nice place you have. Good decorator."

She lifted one eyebrow and turned before she poured. "I did it myself."

The crooked grin became a rueful smile. "I just keep putting my foot in it, don't I?"

She poured carefully, then replaced the pitcher in the refrigerator. Grasping both glasses, she turned. "You can't help making snap judgments, I suppose." She handed him a glass. "You assume you know me, assume I'm just part of a group who behave in a predictable way. But you don't know me, Dev." She met his gaze evenly, her stomach burning from her daring.

He looked into his glass. "I'm finding that out." He fixed his eyes on her again. "Listen, Lacey, about the park—"

"Forget it, Dev. It's over."

Green eyes darkened. "I shouldn't have kissed you."

Suddenly, her sunny kitchen became crowded with memory, shadowed by the past. "Please, Dev. Don't." *I can't talk about any of it. I can't bear it.*

"But—" He stopped and studied her closely.

She waited for an eternity, praying he wouldn't continue. She didn't know how to be around him, how to forget, how to proceed. How to cover the maelstrom he generated inside her.

Dev exhaled sharply, then nodded. "All right. But I am sorry. I'd like to make it up to you. If that's possible. You don't know it, but that wasn't like me. I don't—" He caught her look. "All right, I'll stop. But I would like to show you that I know how to behave. Let me take you to dinner."

"I'm sorry. I have plans. My parents are having a party tonight—" And thank God for that. How would she make it through an entire evening with him?

"A rain check, then?"

This was Dev, but it wasn't. This man was far more serious, far less reckless. Time had wrought changes in them both. He'd had pride, even when he had nothing else. Could she trade his pride for her comfort and like herself?

She was her mother's daughter. She'd weathered many difficult occasions with a smile firmly in place. Dev would be her biggest challenge, but a part of her wanted to try.

"All right. But you live in Dallas, right?"

That killer smile returned. "It's only three hours, and I'm in and out of Houston on business all the time."

Suddenly memory and shadows fled, and he was simply a very attractive man asking her for a date.

Maybe they could do this. Maybe it wouldn't be as hard as she feared.

He chuckled. "I see second thoughts. I promise I'll be on my best behavior. Scout's honor." He held up three fingers.

Lacey had to smile at that. "You were never a Boy Scout, Devlin Marlowe."

He chuckled. "Ouch."

The moment spun out on a filament of shared laughter. Something inside her chest eased just a little.

The doorbell rang. Lacey glanced at the clock. "Oh, dear. I'm late. My parents are throwing their annual cocktail party for half of Houston." She knew she was babbling, but that would be Philip at the door.

"Dr. Blondie, I presume?" Dev cocked one dark eyebrow in challenge.

Lacey stifled her grin, setting her glass down hastily. "I'm sorry, Dev. You'll have to excuse—"

Philip walked in the front door without waiting, his glance darting between the two of them. "It was unlocked. You didn't answer."

Lacey straightened carefully, her hand settling against her stomach. "Hello, Philip," she said brightly. "I'm sorry. I'm running late."

Dressed for the party, he took in her appearance, his gaze sharp. "So I see." He fastened on Dev, his face turning hard. "I don't believe we've met. Dr. Philip Forrester." He extended his hand.

Lacey felt caught between two warring stallions. The atmosphere crackled with challenge.

"Devlin Marlowe." Dev shook his hand firmly but didn't explain his presence. Inside the man, she could still see the rebellious teen, chin jutting forward.

Philip seemed taken aback, but he covered it smoothly. "Lacey, you'll need to get ready. We'll be late." He turned toward Dev, smooth and urbane. "You must be the fellow who bought my fiancée's basket."

She wanted to strangle him.

"And you're the loser," Dev answered.

Lacey wanted to laugh. Or strangle Dev, too. Hastily, she intervened. "Dev was just returning the basket. I forgot it."

Philip turned his attention from her to Dev. "Well, that's done now. I suppose you'll be leaving."

Dev didn't answer him. He turned toward Lacey, taking her hand and kissing her knuckles like a brand of possession. "I'm sorry I made you late for your party, Lacey. I'll call you soon." His mouth burned her everywhere he touched her skin.

Philip looked as though he might explode, but his impeccable manners kept him frozen in place.

"I don't think you'll need to be doing that. Lacey doesn't date. We're going to be married."

Dev looked up at her, his green eyes bright with a devilish glint. One eyebrow lifted. He squeezed her hand, then turned toward Philip. "That's not what Lacey says."

An unhealthy red rose in Philip's face. His jaw hardened, his eyes sparking fire.

As soon as she got her breath back from the shivers chasing down her spine, she'd never speak to either one of them again. She cleared her throat. "Thank you for returning the basket, Dev. Now if you'll excuse me, I'll see you out and go get ready." She could barely see the sofa ahead of her for the red haze edging over her vision.

Thank heaven he complied—finally. With an audacious wink, he left.

Lacey resisted the urge to slam the door. She drew a deep breath and turned to face Philip.

"What the devil was he talking about, Lacey? This is an outrage," he spluttered.

"I have to get ready, Philip. You know how Mother gets. We'll have to discuss this later." *Maybe there'll be a hurricane. Maybe time will stop. Maybe I'll never have to try to explain what just happened. I don't know, myself.*

Without waiting for Philip's answer, Lacey raced for her bedroom, cursing men in general.

If he had a damn suit with him, he'd crash the party. Maybe he would, anyway.

Then the look on Lacey's face rose up before Dev again, and he shook his head. No matter how he wanted to punch that supercilious jerk in the face, it wasn't fair to put her under that pressure.

The memory of her delicate hand pressing her stomach intervened. As a girl, Lacey had tried so hard—too hard—to be perfect. To be everything that was expected of her. With her parents, *everything* was a crushing burden.

It had taken careful wooing years before to break her free. And in the end, he discovered he hadn't freed her at all. It had been an illusion.

But he could still remember her breathless shock and exhilaration the first time he'd helped her sneak out of her house. There had been a risk-taker locked up inside the princess—

But was there still?

You're on a case, Dev. This is a job. You're here to figure out the best way to break the news, then do it and get the hell out of Dodge. As he sat in his car tucked away just down the block from her town house, waiting for her and Dr. Blondie to emerge, Dev wondered what he thought he was doing.

But all the sleepless nights since the picnic made him edgy and reckless again. Made him want to forget the Gallaghers, forget the case, forget—

Betrayal.

The thought sobered him. Why should he feel protective toward her? She hadn't stood up for him. He'd been on a bus the next morning, headed for basic training, and the next two years had made a hard man out of a boy. He'd done his stint, come back to Houston and worked like a dog until he could move the whole family to Dallas.

Then he'd worked like a dog again.

What did the princess know of hard times? She'd chosen this life of ease over his love, and she was welcome to it. Dev reached for the ignition switch, ready to leave for Dallas, though he'd just driven in this afternoon.

A movement at the door of Lacey's town house grabbed his attention. As the couple emerged, he could see the tension between them, the way Forrester's jaw was locked, his face hard. He had a tight grip on Lacey's elbow—

And she had her hand on her stomach again.

Damn it all. He had no right to intervene, but he wanted to smash his fist in Forrester's face.

Stand up for yourself, Lacey. Come on. You can do it.

Then Dev subsided. He'd caused this trouble, calling Forrester a loser. Flinging it in his face, questioning their involvement.

He watched Lacey's grace as she settled into the luxury sedan, long, slender legs emphasized by the high heels. A simple sleeveless black cocktail dress with a strand of pearls spoke of restrained elegance, of a fit that only money could buy.

She looked delicate and ethereal, somehow unapproachable and remote. Dev could make killings in the stock market until he turned blue, and he'd still be the kid from the wrong side of the tracks. Wrong for her.

He'd tail them, just to make sure she was all right. But he'd nip foolish fancies in the bud. She was the princess. He was the peasant. She might not have the blue blood that she thought, but she belonged in this world in a way he never would.

And he still had a job to do. Blasting her world apart as gently as possible.

Jaw rigid, Dev pulled away from the curb, wondering again what the hell kind of magician he thought he was.

Alighting from Philip's car, Lacey spared a quick glance for the wide porch of her parents' home. She'd had childhood tea parties there, gotten her first kiss behind one wide column. This house had been her refuge for all of her life, an existence so sheltered, so different from Christina's.

Before they reached the door, Murphy opened it. "Well, Miss Lacey, haven't seen you in a while." He nodded. The gentle reproof made her feel right at home. Murphy had been delivering lectures since she was tiny. "Dr. Forrester." Murphy's eyes were cooler, looking at Philip. For the first time in years, she remembered that he'd had a soft spot for the young, rebellious Dev.

"Hello, Murphy." She reached up and bussed his cheek, knowing it would unsettle him—and horrify her mother.

It did.

"Hello, Lacey." Margaret DeMille's brows drew together less than a millimeter, but it was enough to convey the message. She stood near the doorway, greeting her guests, trim and straight as ever. She flicked a glance over Lacey's demure little black dress, and her frown eased, just a little.

"Hello, Mother." Lacey crossed the foyer and exchanged air kisses.

Her father turned from another guest, and she was pulled into strong arms. Charles was aging, but he still had the vigor of a younger man. "Princess, you look beautiful, as always. Philip—glad to see you." He shook Philip's hand, then leaned closer to Lacey. "When are you going to let him make an honest woman of you?"

"Daddy," she protested.

Guests nearby chuckled.

"As soon as she'll say yes, Charles," Philip responded. "Your daughter has a mind of her own, it seems." His eyes broadcast anger she hoped no one else saw.

She cast a glance over his shoulder. "Mother's waiting for me to help her, Daddy. I'd better go."

"All right, princess." Her father hugged her and kissed her cheek. She wanted to lean against his strength and let him tell her what to do.

But he'd tell her to marry Philip, and she'd put off dealing with that too long.

"I'll catch up with you soon, darling." Philip's tone said that the subject was far from ended.

Philip was much like her mother. He would never violate their contract of good breeding by making a scene. He, like Margaret, would simply expect Lacey to see the light and behave accordingly. Lacey would be dutiful. Her mother would be proud. Philip was counting on that.

But however much the expectations grated, Lacey was only too aware of how much she had when Christina had so little.

Lacey put on her hostess face and began to mingle.

It must have been three hours later before she could seize a moment to sit down. Her face felt as though it would crack from the effort of constant smiling, and her feet hurt like she'd walked on sharp stones. But Lacey had been raised in a tradition that denied physical discomfort. Beauty knows no pain, her mother always said.

It was another lie, just like many Lacey was beginning to despise.

"There you are," Philip said, drawing her out of one set of the French doors that opened onto the expansive front porch.

Lacey stifled a groan. Here it came. "Hello, Philip. Having fun?"

He cocked one sandy eyebrow, his composure, as ever, unruffled. Nothing about Philip ever got ruffled. His hair was razor cut and wouldn't dare misbehave. He never got a speck of anything on his clothes. And his blue eyes were cold as ice.

She'd never realized that until she'd seen green fire again.

"Lacey, it's time we settled this. There's no reason to delay any longer. It's time for us to marry. You'll be too old soon to have the family we want."

She wouldn't get angry. A lady didn't lose her temper. "Too old?" She kept her face carefully composed. "I don't think thirty-three is exactly ancient, Philip."

"Of course not," he soothed. "You're still very

beautiful.'' His eyes narrowed. ''Not quite ready for a little eye job, even. Soon, though.''

Wrinkles show you've lived. Dev's viewpoint strengthened her resolve.

She kept her expression calm. ''Perhaps I don't want an eye job. Perhaps I want my face to reflect my life.''

His gaze sharpened at the edge in her tone. ''Of course, that's your option. I won't demand that you—''

That did it. ''You demand from me all the time, Philip. You don't value what I do for the children, you've got our life all planned out, and you never listen to one word I say.''

He drew himself up in affront. ''Calm yourself, Lacey. This is an important crowd.''

''Important to whom?'' Unaccustomed anger thrilled through her blood. ''These people know nothing about real life—nothing. This is an artificial world, Philip, and you don't even know that, do you?'' Fury gave her a second wind. ''There are children going hungry tonight, but they're just stories on the news to you, aren't they?''

''Lacey, get hold of yourself.'' He grasped her elbow. ''I told you that silly volunteer work wasn't good for you—''

''Silly! You, who keep rich, bored women looking like they're twenty-five, have the nerve to call what I'm doing silly?''

''Shh, Lacey—'' He cast a glance at the windows, then drew her behind a pillar. ''Is it that Marlowe person who's got you so upset? He's not our type, Lacey. Your father told me about him. He's a born troublemaker, and he took money to abandon you once before—''

Lacey jerked away from him, rage and shame swirling into a witch's brew inside her. How dare her father tell that humiliating story? How dare Philip presume to judge her? To write off what she did as useless and foolish?

She had to get out of here, but Philip would never let her leave alone, not as long as he thought he had a claim on her.

And she could not bear to spend one more second in his company. Time had run out.

''We're not getting married, Philip.''

''What?'' He took a step closer. ''Lacey, you're distraught. You know how high-strung you are. I'll take you home and you'll get a good night's sleep. Everything will look fine tomorrow.''

But certainty flooded her veins. She refused to give a raven-haired bad boy the credit, but Dev's arrival had, at least, made her open her eyes and see that she'd been drifting.

She might not know what she was doing with her life, but she knew what she would not do. But emotion wouldn't sway Philip. Only reason would. ''Philip—'' She forced calm, placing one hand on his arm. ''You don't love me, and I don't love you. And marriage isn't a business arrangement.'' *At least, not for me.* ''We wouldn't make each other happy, Philip. We'd wind up like your parents.''

She had him there. In one of his few moments of unbending, he'd told her how much he'd hated growing up with parents who made every excuse to stay apart, until one day they'd finally split up.

"I don't think you know what you're saying," he murmured. "You should think about it a little longer."

She shook her head. "I won't change my mind. I've been avoiding this for too long, but I knew. I told you, too, Philip. Be honest. I never led you to believe I wanted to marry."

"I thought I could change your mind."

"I'd like to part friends, if we could. And I'll explain to my parents."

"They won't be happy." His mouth was tight.

"No, they won't be happy. You're exactly what they want. It's me who doesn't fit." She'd felt it all her life, but she'd never understood why. She'd tried very hard to bury that sense of displacement, but when she allowed herself to look deep, she saw the girl who did everything perfectly...but didn't feel as if it was ever enough.

Philip's jaw worked as he stared off into the distance. Finally, he exhaled in a long gust, shaking his head. "You're never going to find whatever that romantic fantasy is, Lacey." He turned to face her. "Don't you know that by now? Haven't you made enough mistakes?"

She stiffened. "Apparently not." She forced calm where temper wanted to reign. "I'll tell my parents. You don't have to deal with it."

"Fine," he said curtly, facing the windows. He paused after two steps, speaking over his shoulder. "Is it Marlowe, Lacey? Is he what's gotten you stirred up?"

She recoiled. "Of course not. You think I'd be that foolish after what he did?"

Philip sighed. "Apparently, my judgment isn't to be trusted." He shook his head. "Don't do anything you'll regret. I would still take you back as long as you don't embarrass me." He turned to face her. "Why don't you come inside now? It's getting chilly out here."

Steam could easily pour out her ears after that last little salvo. But lady to the core, Lacey only shook her head. "I'm not your concern anymore, Philip. I'll be inside after a moment."

He shrugged and left.

Lacey looked out onto the estate where she'd spent her life trying to become what other people wanted. Her head felt light from a mixture of grief that she still couldn't quite hit the mark...and relief. Elation. For one second, Lacey imagined what Dev would say if he were here.

She could still remember swallowing almost-hysterical giggles the night he'd helped her climb out of her second-floor window and down the trellis. The incredible euphoria of forbidden thrills as they raced across the lawn, darting from tree to tree to avoid detection. Dev had had to muffle her giggles with his hand because she couldn't hold them back.

Finally, he'd resorted to kisses. Hot, wet, deep, day-long kisses that had turned the champagne-bubbly giggles into moans and sighs.

Suddenly, Lacey knew what she wanted to do. She didn't want to go back inside. She wanted to escape, to run away. To be free for just a little while.

One of the valets would take her home. She

stepped off the porch and walked toward the parking area her father had built near the street. With every step, she felt giddy. Younger. Breathless in a scary, lighter-than-air way.

Devlin Marlowe was a born troublemaker and hardly a good example to follow, but she thought he'd be proud of what she'd done. Too bad he'd never know. If he did call as he'd promised, she wouldn't see him. She had too much thinking to do, and in his own way, Dev was as overbearing as Philip.

But she was a free woman, at least for tonight. She would have to tell her parents soon, but for now, she felt like running.

And so she did, heels and all.

Circling around the neighborhood one last time, Dev was still kicking himself for not leaving her alone. She was a big girl. He shouldn't interfere.

But he just wanted to know that she was all right.

Suddenly, he saw a form hurtle through the darkness, stopping to engage in intent conversation with a valet.

It couldn't be. But it was. Lacey was gesturing, and the valet was lifting his shoulders. Her own frame sank in disappointment.

Dev started his car and rolled slowly toward her, letting down the passenger window.

"Hey, lady, need a ride?"

The valet started to protest, but Lacey turned and spotted him.

Her smile blossomed. "He's a friend," she explained to the valet who was still busy urging her to return to the house. "Thank you so much for your help." She turned to Dev. "Do you have any money?"

Dev retrieved a twenty and handed it to her.

Lacey gave it to the flustered valet. "Please simply tell Dr. Forrester that I've gone home with a headache. And tell my parents I'll talk to them later. Tell them I took a cab, all right?"

The man shrugged, then walked away, muttering.

Lacey opened Dev's door. "I'm not going to ask what you're doing here. Just drive, okay?"

Dev studied the odd, febrile excitement on her face. "Well, I am going to ask. What are you doing, Lacey?"

She placed a hand on her stomach, then drew a deep, ragged breath. She turned to him, her voice a little shaky but her smile growing wider by the moment. "I think I'm making a jailbreak."

Dev was so surprised, he laughed out loud. "You sure you want to do this?"

She breathed deeply again, shaking her head. "I don't want to think." But then she grinned, and it was like a full moon breaking through the clouds. "But I didn't have to climb down a trellis this time. Now will you please get me out of here—fast?"

"You got it, lady." Dev hit the pedal hard, and his tires screeched.

Lacey clapped her hands together, three quick claps in succession. He heard a small squeal erupt from her throat, then dissolve into nervous laughter. "I just got formally unengaged—not that I ever agreed in the first place. My mother will be furious."

But she looked slightly delighted.

"Where to?" he asked.

"I should go home...." A faint frown appeared.

He waited for her upbringing to assert control.

"Is that what you want?" It would be the smart thing—but not, he realized, what he wanted. "Or is it what you think you should do?"

Lacey glanced at him. Across her features, indecision chased worry...hard on the heels of temptation.

"I probably should—" Then she smiled. "But I don't want to."

He shouldn't feel this kick in his pulse. He'd left the rebel behind years ago, he'd thought.

Maybe he'd thought wrong.

"A jailbreak calls for a celebration, I think," Dev said. "And I know just the place to toast a formal unengagement that never existed in the first place, as long as you like your coffee strong and hot."

Her head whipped around. "You do?"

Dev nodded. "You're in good hands. Settle back and enjoy the ride."

"Dev?"

Here it came. Second thoughts.

"Can we put the top down?"

Surprise made him grin. "Sure—but your hair won't be the same." He pulled over in the parking lot of a dry cleaner.

"But that's like wrinkles, right? Just makes things interesting?" She turned suddenly to study him. "Philip thinks I'm almost ready for an eye job."

Dev cursed vividly under his breath as he fastened down the top. "Philip is an ass. What did you ever see in him, anyway?"

"It wasn't me. It was my parents."

Dev came back and slid into the driver's seat. He thought about chiding her, but she'd never been any different. Too eager to please a father who didn't deserve her love.

But he didn't need to get started thinking about Charles DeMille. Or the past.

And anyway, he had to give her credit for making a jailbreak tonight. He started up the car again.

She ran slender fingers through her hair and stretched her arms above her head, turning her head side to side as the wind whipped her and plastered her dress to her curves.

Dev bit back a groan. She looked like a woman in the throes of passion.

This is a bad idea, Dev. Ba-a-ad idea. Take her home.

"So where are we going, Devlin Marlowe?"

"I'll take you to a place where your friends won't see you. Somewhere you'd never dream of setting foot inside."

"I don't care if my friends see me," she protested.

Don't lie to me—or yourself, Lacey. You care.

But he didn't say that. "You're gonna weep over Shorty's doughnuts."

Lacey smiled back, crossing her arms over her chest. "Prove it."

Dev chuckled. "You asked for it, darlin'. Now

hang on.'' Averting his eyes, he shot the car forward, concentrating on the road ahead of them and trying his damnedest not to think about the woman at his side.

Chapter Six

Dev pulled to a stop in front of the darkened building in a decaying part of Houston. Lacey's quick glance made him smile as he turned to her. "It's okay, I promise. It's just run-down, not dangerous."

Her chin tilted upward. "I wasn't—"

Dev grinned. "Yes, you were. I'd bet a hundred bucks you've never been near this part of town before."

In the light from the street lamp, he could see her shoulders stiffen. "Of course I—" Her voice trailed off. Lacey sighed. "You're right, I haven't."

"Rethinking your jailbreak? I can take you back right now. They might not even realize you're gone."

There was enough heat in the look she shot him

to melt lead. Dev wanted to applaud, but he was still waiting for her to realize that she didn't belong here. Not with him. Not anywhere near him.

"I'm not going back," she countered. "Now do I get my doughnuts or not?" She peered out of the windshield. "What is this place anyway?"

"Shorty's place is in back. It's a deep, dark secret. I probably should have blindfolded you first." He grinned. "I'd give you the password and secret handshake, but then I'd have to kill you."

Lacey burst out laughing. Slowly, she drew an X over her heart. "I swear I won't tell. Besides," she muttered, "I'm not sure I could find this place again if my life depended upon it."

Her laughter touched places in him that felt... undiscovered. Untouched. Almost young again.

What the devil was he doing, showing her one of his favorite haunts? She would come to her senses anytime now, realize just how different they were and demand to be taken back. And Shorty's would never be the same refuge.

But they were here. If she did—when she did— he'd deal with it. But that was later. This was now. "When you taste Shorty's doughnuts, you'll be forever marked. You'll be able to find your way back like a homing pigeon. These doughnuts change you at the cellular level."

"Hip level, you mean."

It took a minute for her remark to register. He laughed. "You're too skinny, anyway. A few extra pounds won't hurt you."

For a second, what might have been hurt raced

over her features. "If I'm too thin for you, that's not really my problem, Devlin."

Ah, princess to peasant. Back on familiar ground.

"You're beautiful and you know it. I'm just saying there's nothing wrong with a woman's hips being curvy. You're not supposed to look like a boy. Your body was built to make babies."

She went silent for too long.

Dev swore silently. "I'm sorry. I don't mean—" Hell, he should just quit talking. He never had the right words with her.

Then she touched his hand with her fingers, lightly. "It's okay. I was just…thinking. You're right, you know. The circles I move in, well… I think we've gotten a long way from the basics." She glanced down. "I forget that sometimes—that fitting into this season's size four isn't what nature designed my body to do."

When she looked up, there was something fragile in her face. Dev wanted way too much to take her in his arms right then. "Do you want children, Lacey?"

"Oh, yes," she said softly. Her look turned inward.

"Then why haven't you married by now? Had a dozen kids? I can't imagine you haven't been asked—" He tried for a grin. "Even before Dr. Blondie."

She looked down at the hands clasped tightly in her lap. "I was married, once." Then she frowned, grasped the door handle and stepped outside.

Dev followed her lead, rounding the car and coming to stand before her. He knew about the marriage, of course, but only that it had been annulled, not why. He kept his tone gentle. "Can I ask what happened?"

She shot him a sideways glance he couldn't decipher. "I made a mistake." A look of immense sadness swept over her face.

Dev gripped her shoulders. "Maybe he didn't deserve you."

Her head rose as shock tripped across her features.

Just as quickly, the Margaret DeMille mask dropped into place. She shrugged elegantly and stepped back. "It was a long time ago." Then Lacey glanced around them. "I don't see any doughnuts, but I could swear I smell them."

Let it be, Dev. Just a job, remember?

But that didn't seem to stop him from wanting to hold her. To do whatever it took to erase the sadness that dogged her when she didn't have her mask fully on. To protect her from her own vulnerability.

But if he couldn't give her comfort, he could at least give her doughnuts. He crooked his arm. "This way, madam." He leaned down and waggled his eyebrows. "But the chocolate ones are mine."

Lacey took his arm, and her smile almost reached her eyes. "Not if I get there first."

Dev led her down the side of the building to a nondescript door. He knocked five sharp raps, then waited. Lacey looked at him curiously, but he merely shrugged. "He'll get here, don't worry."

As if he were prophetic, the door opened just then. Shorty's broad smile peered out of his grizzled, coffee-colored face. "Well, bless my soul, if you ain't a sight for sore eyes." Then he caught a glimpse of Lacey and whistled low. "Dev, my man, you comin' up in the world. Mornin', ma'am." He tipped an imaginary hat.

Margaret DeMille would freeze Shorty dead for such familiarity. To Dev's relief, Lacey only smiled shyly. "I guess it is close to morning, isn't it? Are you really making doughnuts at this hour, you poor man?"

Shorty shot a glance at Dev. "Hear that, boy? 'Poor man.' The woman has proper respect for my hard work, unlike some people I know." He winked at Lacey and held out his arm. "My name is Shorty, ma'am. Come along and I'll treat you to the best doughnuts that ever hit your tongue."

To her credit, Lacey only hesitated a second, then took his arm as if they were old friends. "Please call me Lacey—" She smiled back at Dev, the devil in her eyes "—and I like chocolate doughnuts best."

Dev stopped dead in his tracks when she stuck out her tongue at him. He laughed out loud.

"Then ol' Dev's luck just ran out 'cause I'll feed a beautiful woman every chocolate doughnut in the place. You go on back to the car now, Dev. Me and your lady, we've got some fat to chew, most of it about how bad her judgment is, bein' here with a young rascal like you. She needs a mature man to treat her right."

Dev snorted. Shorty was mature all right—seventy if he was a day. A comeback was on his lips—

When Lacey giggled.

Giggled. Like a teenage girl. When she glanced back at him, her eyes sparkled.

Dev could only stand there, holding the door in wonder. He'd half-expected to shock her by bringing her here—instead she was stealing his doughnuts.

His heart lightened, and he moved to follow them. "Oh, no, you don't—you're not giving away my doughnuts, Shorty. She can't even find her way back here without help."

Shorty snorted as they walked. "She won't need to if she'd run away with me and leave your sorry butt behind."

Lacey giggled again. Shorty's deep chuckle joined her as he brought her through the door to his domain, seating her with a flourish at the scarred table Dev had haunted for many a dawn when he was a kid throwing papers.

"Go turn that batch, Dev, while I make this pretty lady some fresh coffee."

Dev saw Lacey's surprised glance and shrugged. "I spent half my teenage years here, helping Shorty make doughnuts in return for all I could eat."

Shorty called back. "The boy had a hollow leg. Ate twice as many as he ever made, I promise you that. Snitched more when he thought I wasn't lookin', then headed out on that paper route early every mornin'."

Lacey looked surprised again. "You were a paperboy?"

"Yeah." Dev waited for it to sink in that after his father's death, he had lived not far away, in a part of town where she wouldn't be caught dead after dark.

Instead she rose and came to stand beside him, watching. "Was it hard, having to get up so early? What about school?"

The last thing he wanted was to discuss those years with her. He pointed to the doughnuts floating in the boiling grease. "Better stand back. This can splatter on you."

But Lacey just moved closer, watching him turning two at a time as Shorty had taught him. "May I try turning one?"

Dev shot her a glance. She was serious. He shook his head. "That dress is too expensive to ruin."

"The handles are long enough. I'll be careful." She glanced up at Shorty. "May I?"

Shorty was watching both of them, his look assessing Dev as much as Lacey. "Don't know why not. Show the lady how it's done, boy."

Dev glanced around, saw Shorty's spare apron hanging nearby. With quick steps, he snatched it down and returned to slip it over Lacey's head, then stood behind her, realizing it was far too big for her.

So he wrapped the strings around her narrow waist twice, then tied them behind her, the rich scent of her perfume tracing through the sugar-laden air.

And he recognized that his hands were unsteady with the need to touch the sweet line of her hips, to pull her back against him and bury his face in her hair, to kiss her nape.

Shaken, he glanced up and saw sympathy in

Shorty's eyes. It pulled him back to what was real, what made sense. He didn't know this Lacey who had layers and hidden depths, and the bald fact was that he probably never would.

But tell that to the rebel inside who had never cared very much what was sensible—or forbidden to him.

He pulled her back slightly to his left side, shielding her with his body while he demonstrated the fine art of judging when a doughnut is done. He pulled two out, flipped them neatly into the chocolate glaze, then went back for more. Then he reached for the first two and flipped them up on the shelf above, where the glaze dripped back into the pan. Then he handed the sticks to Lacey.

She worried at that lush lower lip with her teeth while she concentrated, and Dev was hard-pressed to pay attention to the doughnuts. She executed the first two perfectly, her smile of triumph real and bright. When she turned toward him to exult, her breasts brushed lightly against his arm, and Dev felt it all the way down to his bones. She froze but she didn't move away, her gaze locked on his.

Shorty's voice cut through the haze. ''Coffee's done.''

Dev and Lacey all but leaped apart. Dev cleared his throat and turned back to the dough. ''If we want more, we'd better get cracking. Shorty does his the old-fashioned way, and he'll have people standing in line when morning comes.''

A tiny frown winked between her elegant brows. Dev saw the confusion in her eyes and wished he could make himself walk away from her right now.

There was nothing confused about his body's response to hers, nothing at all.

His mind was another matter altogether. *Light and easy, Dev. Remember who she is, who you are. What she did.*

So he busied himself finishing a batch for them, studiously trying to forget that she stood a heartbeat away. Then they each loaded a stack of paper towels with the fruits of their labor and moved to the table where two cups of coffee sat, leaving Shorty behind to go on with his work.

Dev watched her closely as she took her first bite of a doughnut almost too hot to touch.

Lacey closed her eyes in bliss, moaning softly. Dev's body tightened at the sound. Then those witchy silver eyes opened, and she licked her lips. "That is the single best thing I've ever tasted in my life. Pure, raw sin. It surely must be illegal."

Her smile was little short of wicked. "I'm going to eat at least a dozen." She took another bite, and a breathy sigh escaped.

One glistening drop of chocolate lingered at the corner of her mouth. Dev fought the bittersweet temptation to lean across and kiss the chocolate away.

Instead, he forced himself to take a bite of his own, but it might as well have been sawdust for all he knew of what he was eating.

It didn't matter, though. He'd eaten a thousand of Shorty's doughnuts. Lacey's delight was more than enough.

So they talked and drank coffee and ate more doughnuts than either could count. Shorty popped over and visited between batches, but mostly Dev and Lacey talked about everything under the sun.

Everything, that is, but themselves, perhaps she as eager as he to avoid the mine field of their past, of the differences between them. She kept their breakfast talk superficial, switching topics with the ease of an accomplished hostess...but as time wore on and the first touch of giddiness faded, she inched back into being more Margaret DeMille's daughter than the woman who'd run across the lawn in high heels. He wished he could figure out how to bring the jailbreak girl back.

Then the first deliveryman showed up, and they could hold back the knowledge no longer. The magic island of the night was vanishing as dawn approached.

In silence, Lacey rose and worked at the ties of her apron, but Dev could see that his hasty knot was about to defeat her. "Here, let me." He turned her back toward him and tried to maintain his distance. The ball was over...and he was about to turn back into a pumpkin.

His fingers grew clumsy, and it took him far too long. He could tell by her rigid posture that the real world was sinking back into Lacey's consciousness too fast, the knowledge of what she'd done at last hitting her.

"Just a minute more," he muttered, and wished they had hours. Finally she was free and he had no excuse to touch her again.

As she lifted the apron over her head, she avoided his gaze. "I'll take this back to Shorty."

He could only stand and watch.

Lacey spoke with Shorty for a few moments, then lifted to tiptoe and kissed his cheek. Behind her back, Shorty smiled sadly at Dev.

He saw it, too.

In a reverse kind of Cinderella story, the almost-real girl who'd laughed with them…was turning back into a princess.

On the drive back, Lacey sat still and quiet, and Dev could think of no way to bring back the ease of those few precious hours.

Pulling into her drive, Dev knew he shouldn't have done it. He had only complicated things more by stealing her away, by discovering that she could be real. That she had a clever sense of humor carefully hidden under all those layers of politeness.

Lacey might not understand it, but far more deadly than her beauty was the giggle that should have belonged to a teenage girl. Something had happened inside his chest each time he heard it.

Damn. He liked her.

That was something he'd missed the first time around. He'd started out using her to get revenge on her father, then fallen too quickly into hormone-drenched teenage lust. Somehow, the desire for revenge had faded as lust had turned to something more tender when he wasn't looking.

He'd never taken the time to find out if they could be friends before his revenge had turned its blade and skewered him. Now, of course, friends were all they could be—at least, until he found the right way to break the news without breaking her heart.

He was more certain than ever that she didn't know the secret that could explode her whole world. Being a DeMille was something so intertwined with who she was that she never lost sight of it.

But he had to hand it to her. Even when faced with something like Shorty's place, she hadn't turned a hair, had been gracious and warm to Shorty himself. She continued to surprise him.

Yet now she seemed to be absorbing the impact of what she'd done. What she'd thrown away. As he stopped the car, the transformation was complete.

And he hated it.

"Well—" Lacey turned to him, extending one elegant hand. "Thank you for breakfast."

He resisted the urge to growl and ignored her hand. "Sure thing. Anytime you want to go slumming, princess, just give me a call. I know all the dives."

Hurt skipped across her features. She turned away quickly, grasping the door handle. "I'd better go inside."

The more composed she got, the more Dev fumed. He wished he could cancel this damn job, but he didn't trust anyone else to do it. Dev wanted to turn back the clock, get back the woman who'd made a jailbreak, who'd turned doughnuts with glee.

He shouldn't want that. This was business, and damned complicated business at that. He was here to deliver a message, that was all. There was probably no painless way to deliver it, so maybe he should quit trying.

Or maybe he would just let Maddie and Boone show up on her doorstep, after all. Turn this over to them and walk away.

Like hell, he would.

With a hard jerk, he opened his own door and rounded the front bumper of his car to open hers. He extended a hand to her. She hesitated, and he reached in to grasp her hand.

And this time he let his touch linger.

Lacey slid her legs out, the movement lifting the slim black skirt up high on her shapely thighs. Dev stifled a groan and jerked his glance to her face.

"Dev, I—" Nerves jittered in her gaze.

Inside him, something twisted. He took pity on her. "It's not too late to go back, Lacey. Dr. Blondie would still take you in a heartbeat, I'm sure."

She studied him silently, her eyes huge and dark. "I don't want to go back," she said softly. "I'm just not sure where forward is."

He closed his eyes in pain. It didn't seem to matter what he knew was smart. He wanted to protect her, to hold her. To kiss her again.

He almost did it, almost reached out and pulled her into his embrace.

But from somewhere inside the bad boy rose a gentleman who knew that he would only complicate her life more if he did. Charles DeMille would stop at nothing to keep them apart. She still had to get through DeMille's displeasure at the broken unengagement. If Forrester had said anything at all to her parents about finding Dev at her town house, it was Lacey who would suffer for it.

It was the absolute worst time to want to get closer to her. He needed to back away, get some distance. Tonight had confused the hell out of him.

He would leave her alone for a few days, keep an eye on her from a safe distance just to be sure no one was making life too hard. Let her get past this rough spot, then he'd break the news as kindly as possible. Maybe he'd take her to Morning Star himself. That was it, *finito*. That was all he could afford to think about now, no matter what this night had made him want.

To strengthen his resolve, he reminded himself that Lacey needed a friend now, far more than anything else. She looked as alone as anyone he'd ever seen.

But he couldn't leave her like this. Before he stopped to think it through, he spoke up. "Go out with me, Lacey."

Her head jerked around. "What?"

She didn't have to look so incredulous. But he persisted. "Forrester said you don't date. But now you can. It doesn't have to be a *date* date, just friends out for a night on the town. I still owe you that dinner for winning the bet." He was making this up as he went, part of him staring in stunned silence.

Just shut up, he told the stunned part, the part clinging to remnants of sense. The part she'd abandoned once before.

"It'll get you back in the swing of things. Dr. Blondie will tell everyone he dumped you, you know that. Show the world you're doing fine without him."

"Dev, I don't think—"

The past crowded his throat. Remembered rage at a boy's helplessness and humiliation. "What's the matter? Afraid Daddy won't like it?"

Her eyes clicked into defiance. "I don't care about that."

You did once. Too much. Dev could feel temper licking at the edges of his control. "Never mind." He turned to head toward her front door.

Lacey grabbed his arm. "You think I'm such a coward, don't you? How dare you? You don't know me. You never did."

The night brought one more discovery. Lacey had a temper.

Her eyes might be spitting fire now, but his weren't far from igniting, either. "Then prove it. Prove that you're not going to live the rest of your life trying to become your mother."

If she'd had a knife, he'd be bleeding right now. "Name the date." That delicate jaw could crunch rocks at this moment.

"I'll be back next Friday. I'll pick you up at seven."

"Fine," she snapped.

He took the keys from her hand and unlocked the door. "Fine, then. I'll see you on Friday." He stepped aside.

She steamed past him. Suddenly, almost like a marionette, she stopped. "Thank you for the doughnuts."

Damn those perfect manners. Dev gritted his teeth and started to respond.

Lacey slammed the door in his face.

Dev heard the lock click and stood there for a moment, glaring at the closed door. Then the absurdity of it all hit him. Like a madman, he stood on the porch of Lacey's exclusive town house—

And laughed his fool head off.

She was right. He sure as hell didn't understand her. But she fascinated him more every time she crossed his path.

Chapter Seven

Dev headed toward his younger brother Connor's apartment, shaking his head slowly. It was only Wednesday, and he'd sworn to leave Lacey alone this week. But every day she'd been in his thoughts, and he'd worried about how she was doing. When one of his investigators had casually mentioned that he needed to interview someone in Houston, Dev had jumped at the chance to go in his place.

He'd been out of his mind to invite her out for Friday, and here he was, two days early. Knowing already that he wouldn't stay away that long.

She betrayed you, thickhead. Turned her back and chose the life she has. The message had been clear years ago. Marlowes were not good enough for DeMilles.

But the more he saw of Lacey, the more his instincts stirred. The woman he was learning to know had a tender heart. The boy Dev had been wounded to the core that she hadn't chosen him, but that boy had been proud and too ready to leap at the first offense. He'd expected a lot from a sheltered girl.

His plan to even the score with Charles DeMille by seducing the perfect daughter had backfired in his face.

She'd walked away from him, and he'd wound up on the next bus out of town, determined to come back and take his family away from Houston—and Charles DeMille—forever.

He'd done it, put his siblings through college, bought his mother a house, built a lucrative business. Now that he'd become successful, plenty of women considered him only too suitable. He wondered if they would be around if he'd still been poor.

But none of them had been a woman who wanted to take on three kids and an alcoholic mother. Nor one who understood his drive to climb up from poverty and become so successful that no one would ever again say he wasn't good enough.

Lacey wouldn't be any different, would she? She'd cut and run before. He'd made it out of the cesspool, on his own terms. So why the devil was he racing back toward the woman who had been part and parcel of the most painful period of his life?

Dev didn't have an answer that made any sense. So he simply drove.

* * *

"Lacey, darling, are you feeling well?" her mother asked that night at dinner.

It had been a hard week. She'd just found out from Christina's social worker that an unknown aunt had popped up, wanting custody. The social worker suspected that state aid money was the aunt's real goal, and Christina's distress at the news had made Lacey wish she could take the child away and hide her so that no one would ever hurt her again.

On top of that, Lacey hadn't yet had the chance to discuss Philip with her parents, and she'd been dreading it. Nonetheless, she finished her bite and nodded. "Yes, I'm just fine."

"Sure nothing's wrong, princess?" her father inquired.

"No, I—" She took a deep breath to settle herself. Christina's plight had made her resolve to do this before they delved into the painful subject of Philip. "I wanted to thank you both."

Her parents looked startled. "For what?"

"I simply wanted to tell you that I appreciate how lucky I am to have grown up here, to have been born to two people who love me, to—" She was going to cry if she didn't watch out.

Her mother looked uneasy. Her father set his napkin aside, frowning. "What brought this on?"

Lacey looked away, blinking rapidly. With effort, her voice brightened. "I'm fine, Daddy."

"It's that volunteer work, isn't it?" Her mother's incisive gaze sharpened. "I told you, Lacey, that world is not where you need to be. There are better places for you to put your efforts."

Her father nodded agreement. "Princess, I know you want to help those who need it, but isn't there something easier you could do?"

Remembering the little blond girl who'd fallen asleep holding her hand, rebellious words rose to Lacey's lips. Carefully, she drew a deep breath before answering.

"I'm almost thirty-three years old. When am I going to make my life count, if not now?"

"You could make your life count. You could have children by now, Lacey darling, if you would just say yes to Philip," Margaret chided.

"I don't love Philip."

"Bah—" Her father waved it away. "You can grow to love him. That's romantic folderol. You're very well-suited. Know the same people, like the same things."

A sharp retort rose to her lips, but a lifetime's habits didn't vanish in an instant. Lacey rubbed one hand across her stomach and took another deep breath. She had come here to thank them for caring for her so well. They were simply trying to do the same thing now.

But though Philip had apparently not told them anything, she couldn't put this off any longer.

"I'm not going to marry Philip, Daddy. I've already told him that."

"What?" Her parents exchanged sharp glances.

"Lacey, how could you? What more could you want?" her mother asked.

I want more. I want—

What did she want?

Someone who would love her if she were poor

and in rags. The vine-covered cottage, maybe, much as it was maligned.

Someone who saw inside her and didn't care about her name or her face or her bank account.

Someone to love Lacey and let her be herself. To make her feel like she belonged and wasn't hiding behind a mask.

"I want love, Mother. Real love."

"It's Marlowe, isn't it?" Her father's face was thunderous. "He was never any good. Now he's trying to ruin your life again."

"Again?" her mother echoed. "What does that mean?"

Lacey and her father exchanged glances. Her mother hadn't questioned Lacey's sudden acquiescence to Margaret's desire for Lacey to attend finishing school in Europe all those years ago. Lacey had often suspected that her father hadn't divulged what he'd found that night. Her mother would have taken it badly.

She remained silent. It would be his story to tell.

"Nothing, Margaret. I simply didn't like young Marlowe paying too much attention to Lacey when she was so young."

"I told you not to put him to work around here. He was not supposed to go near her. His father was a criminal, after all." Her mother turned to her. "Darling, you can't possibly be involved with that hoodlum."

"He's not a hoodlum, Mother. He's a successful businessman." She swallowed hard. "And we're not involved."

Her mother's laser-sharp eyes studied her, clearly not believing what she said.

Her father spoke first. "You know what he did before." The air went still and dark with memory. Dev had taken money to walk away. Her father's eyes bored into hers. "He cannot be trusted."

Maybe not. Probably not. But a small voice inside her said differently.

But it was none of their business. "This is not about Dev. This is about me, about my life."

"Lacey, I refuse to let you fall victim to him again," her father commanded. "Wasn't Luc lesson enough? Do I have to bail you out every time you show poor judgment?"

Every word drove a stake into her heart. Both their faces were set and angry. Her stomach twisted.

But within Lacey, a tiny seed sprouted. The seed that remembered riding down the highway with the top down in an old Caddy. Climbing down a trellis. Making doughnuts.

She liked that Lacey. She didn't want to bury that Lacey so deeply that she could never find her.

She pushed back from the table and rose. Voice shaking, she spoke. "I'm sorry you have so little faith in me. I've tried very hard to be what you want, but I never seem to manage it." She looked up at her mother's frown, her father's dark stare. "I love you both, but I cannot live my life for you forever."

"Lacey—" her mother warned.

Her father's visage darkened more. "I'm warning you, princess. Marlowe is no good. You stay away from him, or I'll—"

She forced herself to meet his gaze, her knees trembling, her throat dry as dust. "Or what, Daddy? You'll send me away again?"

She pressed her hands together to stop the shaking. "You don't seem to understand that it doesn't have to be a choice. I can live my own life and still love you both." Then the good little girl emerged once again. "Can't you believe that? Please, can't you let me be who I am and still love me, even if I'm not perfect?"

But all that met her was her mother's silence and her father's stony stare.

"I'll let myself out," she said quietly.

And walked away. Before she could crumble.

Dev knew he was a fool to do it, but as the night deepened, he left Connor's apartment and drove toward Lacey's town house.

At the four-way stop nearest her place, a sporty red convertible zipped through the intersection first.

He knew the driver.

She took the next corner too fast, and he frowned as he followed her. When he arrived at her town house, Lacey emerged from her car, slamming the door and sinking against it, burying her face in her hands.

Dev parked quickly and raced across the grass.

"What's wrong?" he asked.

She raised tear-swollen eyes to his, her face a study in misery. "What are you doing here?" she whispered. But on her face, he saw need.

It didn't matter anymore what had happened in the past. Right now, Lacey needed him. He pulled her into his arms and held her close, murmuring nonsense words as he had once comforted his siblings. Without thinking, he set up a rocking motion, widening his stance so that she nestled between his legs, her face against his neck.

Stroking her back with long, slow strokes, Dev let her cry. She felt good against him, better than she should. Something deep inside Dev felt a click that should have scared him off.

Later, he'd think about it, this sense of rightness, but for now, his attention was solely on her.

When the storm of tears abated, she snuffled and tried to pull away. Dev loosened his grip, but kept her within the circle of his arms.

"I'm sorry." Her voice was low and shaky. She sniffled again, and he dug in his back pocket for a handkerchief, handing it to her.

"Thank you. I'm really sorry."

"Don't apologize. Do you want to talk about it?"

She lifted her face to him, ravaged by tears, and he thought she'd never looked more beautiful.

"No." With a shuddery breath, she went on. "Why are you here, Dev?" Her smile was faint and watery. "Do you plan to be my knight in shining armor every time I'm in trouble?"

Realizing that he wanted that too much shook Dev as badly as anything had in years.

He kept things light. "Galahad Marlowe, at your service. You want to make me a cup of coffee? Or how about a visit to Shorty's? His doughnuts cure a multitude of ills."

Lacey's tremulous smile widened. "I don't want to scare him, the way I look."

Dev cupped her jaw in his hand. "You look beautiful, Lacey."

Her eyes sparked gratitude, but within their depths he saw her devastation.

It was the worst kind of madness, but he wanted to soothe away her pain. So he held her face in his hands and lowered his mouth, brushing a simple, gentle kiss on her lips.

"Oh, Dev—" she sobbed, then gripped his wrists and opened to him, turning the simple kiss into something far deeper.

Dev closed his eyes to reason and sanity and gave himself over to the rush of emotion that swept through him like flames through dry tinder. This was her, the girl he'd never forgotten, the one who'd opened herself to him and granted him the right to be her first.

That he'd been robbed of that chance mattered not at the moment. That she'd had no faith in him and walked away didn't figure. All he could feel, all he could think was that she was here, in his arms. Where she belonged.

He never wanted to let her go again. He tightened his arms around her so fast, so hard, that her breath escaped in a whoosh.

The tiniest sliver of reason tried to surface. But when he tried to recover his mind and pull back, Lacey moaned and slid her arms around his neck, pressing her body against his as though they could become part of one another.

Then, a few doors down, a car door slammed, and Dev and Lacey bolted apart.

Her eyes were huge and dark, her breasts rising with every breath, her lips moist from his.

Dev stared at her and tried to remember that this was all wrong, that the timing couldn't be worse. That he had to walk away. Now.

For an endless moment, they stared at one another, the air around them alive and crackling with hunger and longing. In Lacey's eyes, he saw pain and knew he couldn't walk away from her now. He would pay the piper later.

Dev turned away from her, breathing harshly, and reached inside her car for her purse. Gripping her slender shoulders in one arm, he spoke, his voice rough. "Let's go inside, sweetheart."

Lacey leaned into him and let him lead her inside.

But once there, neither knew what to do. Lacey pulled away from Dev and didn't look at him as she offered. "I'll make coffee. Why don't you wait in here?" She fled down the hall.

Dev waited for a moment, calling himself ten kinds of fool, and eyed the door for escape.

Then he cursed, low and vividly, and threw caution to the wind, striding down the hallway after her.

Lacey's hands were shaking as she tried to fill the grinder with beans. She wasn't sure her legs would hold her. How could she have done that, thrown herself into the arms of the man who'd taken money to leave her once before?

She'd wanted to stay in those arms forever.

Dev's arms felt like the safest place in the world. Like the paradise she'd been banished from just as she'd reached the gates. She'd searched for it ever since.

How could that be?

She spilled grounds all over the counter and dropped her hands helplessly at her sides, blinded by tears.

Was her father right about him? No. *No.* There was an explanation, there had to be. But she couldn't discuss it. That would require telling Dev what had happened tonight. She couldn't bear it.

She hadn't heard Dev come in over the noise from the grinder, but he grasped her shoulders, settled her in the closest chair and began assembling the contents of the pot.

Lacey sank back gratefully. She couldn't stand to think about all that she'd lost tonight.

Once he'd started the pot dripping, he turned around, and the silence was deafening. Lacey could feel his gaze on her, but she couldn't meet it yet. She was drained, feeling like she could sleep for a hundred years.

"You don't need coffee," he said. "You need a good night's sleep."

"I'll be fine." But she felt as if she could fall asleep right in this chair.

As decisively as always, Dev acted. "You're going to bed. We can talk tomorrow. You're done for the night."

And with those words, he swept her up in his arms and strode to her bedroom. Quickly and efficiently, he stripped her like a child, settling her under the covers in her underwear and tucking the comforter close around her neck.

"Will you stay?" she asked, her eyes drifting shut. The storm of emotion had rendered her boneless.

He knelt beside her bed and smoothed her hair. "I don't dare. You need sleep."

"You could sleep with me," she offered, yawning hugely.

Dev chuckled. "Babe, if I'm in this bed with you, there will be no sleeping going on, trust me." He brushed a gentle kiss over her lips and murmured against them. "But Friday night, we're going to have a real date. In the meantime, you get some rest. I'll turn off the coffee and let myself out."

Lacey wasn't sure what she mumbled as she fell headlong into sleep.

Dev swung hard at the punching bag, droplets of sweat blurring his vision. He'd given up on sleep after four restless hours and decided to burn off excess energy at the gym near Connor's apartment, where he was staying on this trip. He'd already been training for an hour.

But nothing was helping.

This job was complicated enough without getting his libido involved. He couldn't hold Maddie off much longer. Hurricane Maddie would be in Houston soon if he didn't give her the sister she so desperately longed to know.

He didn't know what had happened last night, but Lacey was in no shape for a surprise raid by

Maddie. But he, who seldom doubted himself, wondered yet again if he were the right person.

For one second, he remembered the feel of her against him, so delicate, so ravaged. Remembered the rightness, the fierce need to protect her.

But he, and the knowledge he possessed, could do her more harm than anyone. With that thought, Dev threw himself back into his workout with the punching bag.

"Somebody get crossways with you, big brother?" Connor Marlowe's voice broke into his thoughts a few minutes later.

Dev accepted the towel in his brother's hands, wiping down his face and neck. "Just making up for missing a couple of workouts." He studied Connor's blue eyes. "What's wrong?"

Connor raked his fingers through shaggy hair as black as Dev's, a sure sign, if Dev had needed it, that he was troubled. "Why do you think something's wrong?"

"I changed your diapers, buddy. Not much about you I don't know." He grinned. "The other dead giveaway is you being up before noon."

Connor flushed. "I'm not a college kid anymore. I'm a contributing member of society."

"Yeah, but you took the day off. It's six—" Dev squinted at the clock across the gym. "Seven o'clock in the morning. What's up?" He motioned to his water bottle, and Connor squeezed a long stream into Dev's mouth that Dev gulped greedily.

"I really wish you'd quit acting like my father." Traces of Connor's teenage rebellion skipped across his features.

"I practically am your father. So what's up?"

Connor's jaw worked tightly. He was silent for a time. Then he looked up. "I had a fight with Kathleen last night while you were gone."

"Over what?"

"Mom. Kath thinks Mom should move in with you or me. She's afraid Mom won't make it this time, either. I told her to back off. It's easy for her to say—she's in L.A. I mean, you've done enough. Mom will make it or won't, but you deserve your freedom."

Dev wasn't sure he trusted his voice. He couldn't recall the last time someone had come to his defense. Right now, he felt like everything he'd gone through had been worthwhile. He tapped Connor's shoulder with one glove, remembering the little boy who used to crawl into bed with him on stormy nights. In some ways, Connor was the son he'd never had. "I, uh—thanks." Dev cleared his throat. "I mean it."

Then he forced a grin. "Tell you what—while you're duking it out, why don't you tell Dierdre to lay off the matchmaking?"

His brother answered with a smile and a shake of the head. "Not on your life, big brother. I'm grateful, but that's going too far. You're all that stands between me and serious heat."

They both fell silent in the wake of strong emotion. Then Connor looked up, blue eyes sparkling. "Tell me there's no candidate to take you out of the game. I'd like a few more years to play around."

For a treacherous instant, Dev thought about a

fragile sylph in bed fast asleep. Frowning, he shook his head vehemently. Maybe she wasn't just a job anymore, but he was far from ready to discuss her with anyone. So he smiled. "Not a chance, buddy. I'm footloose and fancy-free. You're safe for the foreseeable future."

"Well, now that that's settled, want to go a few rounds?"

"Not unless you just like getting pummeled."

"I could take you."

"You and whose army?"

They both grinned, back on comfortable footing.

"Just because I don't want this pretty face messed up so I'm butt-ugly like you—" Connor's eyes sparkled with mischief. "Besides, there's this girl I promised to take flying. Better get going."

"Running away, eh?" Dev chucked him on the chin. "Go on, Romeo. Have fun in the wild blue yonder."

Connor turned to go, then turned back. "Oh, yeah—I forgot. There's a message for you at the apartment from a guy at some museum. Says it's all set for tomorrow night." He cocked his head. "I didn't know you were an art buff."

Dev smiled. It was the centerpiece of a plan that could blow up in his face, but he felt a kick of excitement. "What you don't know about me could fill an encyclopedia."

"You ever get tired of being the voice of authority?" Connor grinned.

"Never." Dev grinned back. "You looked at those papers yet?"

Connor glanced away. "This weekend, I promise."

"Unless a woman shows up."

Connor laughed. "Hey, I'm the lover." He pointed toward the punching bag. "You're the fighter. To each his own."

Dev threw a mock punch at him. "Go on. I hear romance calling."

"And I'm just the one to answer." Connor waved and ambled off.

Dev watched him go. His little brother would laugh if he could see the butterflies in Dev's stomach over what he had planned.

The date of a lifetime. An evening she'd never forget.

In the dark hours of the night, he'd quit kidding himself that the date meant nothing. He wanted one night to bind her to him enough so that maybe—just maybe—she'd forgive him when he had to tell her that she wasn't who she'd always believed.

Dev had gambled on a lot of things in his life, but nothing that had ever turned him inside out like this.

One night. One roll of the dice.

One chance to give them the night that had been stolen seventeen years ago.

He could only pray it would be enough.

Chapter Eight

Nothing fancy. That's what Dev had said when she'd asked what she should wear on their date. Their real date.

Until he'd called her last night, she'd wondered if she'd dreamed it. Even waking up in her underwear yesterday morning and finding a note telling her the coffeepot was set to go hadn't convinced her that she hadn't imagined his tender treatment, his whispered words about wanting to be in bed beside her.

Lacey shivered slightly as she stared into her closet. Though his hands had been careful and almost impersonal as he'd tended her, his eyes had been anything but.

Hot with promises. Dark with need.

Seeing Dev like that again brought back memories of a long-ago night when her body had cried out for his, when desire had shot past her fears to sear her very soul.

He should have been her first, should have been the one to conclude the lessons he'd begun, lessons that had taught a sheltered girl the meaning of passion.

He walked away, Lacey. He took—

Ruthlessly, she shoved those thoughts away. Maybe he'd done that once, but he was a grown man now. Maybe he regretted what he'd done. Maybe he wanted to make things right—

Maybe she was a fool of the worst kind.

Lacey's fingers trailed across garment after garment as her mind tried to sort through a jumble of feelings.

Maybe she was a fool, but within her, a recklessness was growing. The same seed that had sprouted in defiance of her parents' disapproval was growing again.

She was a grown woman, not a scared sixteen-year-old anymore. And from the mists of memories ruthlessly quashed for years arose one she had buried deep. The look on Dev's face as he'd confronted her father in the gazebo, his eyes and his words pleading with her to run away with him, to believe he'd take care of her.

Dear God. The eyes of a woman saw a different scene. Dev was not the strong, self-assured man then—he'd been a boy, only two years older than her, and he'd faced down her father like a lion protecting his mate.

And she'd walked away. To protect him—or herself?

Lacey blinked and forced herself to concentrate on the clothing arrayed before her. What could she trust of memory and the past?

This was just one night. Maybe she was a fool, but maybe Dev had changed, just as she had. She'd told him that he didn't know her, but the same could be said of her. Regardless of how it might turn out, she wanted to see what would happen.

She wanted one night with Devlin Marlowe, one night where they didn't have to sneak around in the darkness, fearing discovery.

And though she touched her stomach in absent habit, it was as much from butterflies of delight as from the tension that was a tight, hot ball growing larger by the minute.

Resolutely, she shook her head and reached for a hanger.

Dev pulled up in her driveway and wondered for the thousandth time what the devil he thought he was doing.

He hadn't been nervous on a date in years, but his palms were damp and his cast-iron stomach danced.

Could he let her matter this much? How would this all end?

The night could be an unmitigated disaster, no matter how hard he'd worked to make it special.

One night, he asked the fates. *Just let us have this one night to make up for what was stolen from us, regardless of who was at fault.*

Then I'll tell her.

Dev drew in one deep breath and rose from the car, walked to the door and knocked. He'd faced stone-cold killers with less trepidation.

The door swung open, and he could see the nerves jumping in her eyes. The sight calmed him.

But hi was all he could say.

She stepped aside, pulling her princess composure into place. "Hello. Would you care to come in?"

So damn polite he wanted to growl. "If you're ready, let's go."

She nodded stiffly. "All right. Let me get my purse."

As she walked away, he let out a long, low breath. Good God. She was a knockout.

The dress swirled around her ankles, something filmy in a shade he guessed you'd call lavender. It nipped in close to her slender waist, rising to a halter top that showed only the tiniest hint of cleavage and cupped her breasts like a lover's hands. Against her camellia-pale skin, an amethyst hung on a silver chain as dainty as her slender collarbone.

It was plenty for his imagination. And not nearly enough for his eyes.

Lacey, naked in the darkness, the moon silvering her small, perfect breasts.

Dev ground his teeth and wondered if the panties she wore tonight were as tiny as the ones he'd held in his hands back then. She wasn't wearing a bra, he could tell that much.

He closed his eyes and silently counted to ten,

The Silhouette Reader Service™ — Here's how it works:

If offer card is missing write to: Silhouette Reader Service, 3010 Walden Ave., P.O. Box 1867, Buffalo NY 14240-1867

NO POSTAGE
NECESSARY
IF MAILED
IN THE
UNITED STATES

BUSINESS REPLY MAIL
FIRST-CLASS MAIL   PERMIT NO. 717   BUFFALO, NY

POSTAGE WILL BE PAID BY ADDRESSEE

SILHOUETTE READER SERVICE
3010 WALDEN AVE
PO BOX 1867
BUFFALO NY 14240-9952

GET FREE BOOKS and a FREE GIFT WHEN YOU PLAY THE...

Lucky 7

SLOT MACHINE GAME!

Just scratch off the silver box with a coin. Then check below to see the gifts you get!

YES! I have scratched off the silver box. Please send me the 2 free books and gift for which I qualify. I understand I am under no obligation to purchase any books, as explained on the back of this card.

335 SDL C4GW

235 SDL C4GS
(S-SE-OS-08/00)

NAME (PLEASE PRINT CLEARLY)

ADDRESS

APT.#   CITY

STATE/PROV.   ZIP/POSTAL CODE

7	7	7	Worth **TWO FREE BOOKS** plus a **BONUS** Mystery Gift!
🍒	🍒	🍒	Worth **TWO FREE BOOKS**!
♣	♣	♣	Worth **ONE FREE BOOK**!
🔔	🔔	🍒	**TRY AGAIN!**

DETACH AND MAIL CARD TODAY!

inhaling sharply through his nostrils, willing his body to subside.

But despite his discomfort, he wanted to laugh and cheer her on. This was nothing flamboyant for some women—the dress was classy and expensive and could easily be considered demure—but for Lacey, it was little short of a revolution.

Her mother would hate it, and her father would tear his head off if he could read Dev's thoughts now.

Knowing that cheered Dev immensely.

"Ready?" he asked as she walked toward him.

Now that she was close, he could smell her scent and his nostrils flared. He repressed a groan. Something expensive, no doubt, that smelled like mystery and sin.

"You look wonderful," he said.

Her tight face eased as she cut a glance toward him. "Thank you. So do you."

His own attire was simple, a charcoal heather shirt with neck open and sleeves rolled up topping a pair of darker charcoal slacks.

He smiled. "My kid brother said I need to snazz up my wardrobe if I want to attract babes."

Lacey grinned, and some of the tension dissolved. "You have a brother? Does he live here?"

Dev nodded. "Yeah. He's eleven years younger and sometimes I stay with him—when he doesn't have one of *his* babes stashed in his apartment."

"So he's an expert?" she teased.

Dev opened her door and handed her into the car. "He thinks so." He rounded the car and got into the driver's seat.

"So what did he think you should wear?"

"Something sleeveless to show off my boxing muscles." Dev shook his head and started the car. "He's sure that's what women want."

Lacey turned to face him, as fascinated as she was horrified. "Boxing, did you say?"

He glanced her way, then pulled out of her drive. "Yeah. Wanna make something of it?"

Her first instinct was politeness. "Why, no, I—" Then her second instinct took over, Margaret DeMille notwithstanding. Lacey laughed in delight.

"Boxing? Really?"

Dev shot her a grin. "Hey, you knew I was a mongrel. Still game to go out?"

Lacey felt the wind whipping her hair and thought about telling her parents or Philip—or Missy Delavant—that she was going out with a boxer. She laughed again.

She turned and cocked her head, studying the man beside her. Noting the broken nose and seeing the ropy muscles of his arms, remembering the strength of his grip and the concern in his eyes.

"Yes, I'm game." Politeness almost prevented her, but then she asked. "Is that what happened to your nose?"

Dev touched his nose lightly. "I wish. Brawling on a weekend pass, I'm afraid. Not too pretty, is it?"

"I like it," she said. "Gives you character."

He grinned. "I'm starting to get wrinkles, too. Think I should go see Dr. Blondie?"

Then he stopped suddenly. "I'm sorry. I

shouldn't have mentioned him. I guess it went bad with your parents, huh?''

She was quiet for a moment.

"Never mind," he offered.

Lacey remembered his tender care, how good she'd felt in his arms. The brushfire that had ignited.

"No, it's all right. It—it wasn't pretty.''

"You want to talk about it?''

It helped that those mesmerizing green eyes were looking at the road and only occasionally at her. She sighed. "They mean well, and I know they love me. They just—" She searched for a way to express the complicated relationship between herself and her parents.

"I've always felt like there was something not quite right with me, like I can't ever quite do everything right, no matter how hard I try. I've been such a dutiful daughter, but all it's done is to make them less tolerant of the ways I want to be different from them and their whole set.''

Dev glanced over at her. "What ways?''

For some reason, she felt as though she could confide in Dev a thought so secret that she'd never dared voice it, even to herself. "I want to adopt Christina.''

His head whipped around again. "The little girl you told me about?''

She nodded. "I know—it's crazy, not to mention complicated. I'd have to resign as her advocate.''

"So what? If you want it, why can't you do it? Will Daddy yank away your allowance?''

His words hurt so much that she fell silent.

"I'm sorry. I didn't mean that as badly as it sounded. It's just that, as far as I know, you don't have a paying job."

"I know you think I'm unbearably spoiled and pampered." She looked out the window, wondering why she'd ever agreed to come.

He pulled his car into a parking place in the museum district. Turning slightly, he placed on hand on hers. He wouldn't let go when she tried to yank it away. His voice turned soft and soothing. "It was a low blow, Lacey. I guess I've still got some splinters buried in my skin. But you didn't deserve that."

Her shoulders relaxed. "I'm the rich girl. I should be used to it."

He stroked the back of her hand with his thumb. "But you're not, are you?" It was a revelation to him. Her life looked like she had it wired.

She turned to face him, finally. "No, I'm not. I'm really tired of being judged on where I live and what my last name is."

A faint hope stirred in Dev. Maybe she wouldn't hate the news he bore.

Lacey lifted her chin as though making an admission of darkest sin. "I have a trust fund from my grandfather. It's ample for my needs and I feel that my time is better spent giving it to those who have less instead of trying to earn more." She was braced as though waiting for him to laugh.

He clasped her hand tightly and lifted it to his lips. "I think that's admirable."

Her eyes widened. "Really? Not frivolous?"

"I'll bet your friend at the plastic surgeon's office doesn't do anything nearly as hard as working with the advocate's office.''

Lacey smiled. ''You're right. She works as a docent at a museum.''

Dev pressed his lips against her knuckles. ''If you want to adopt that little girl, I say go for it. She'd be damn lucky to have you.''

Her eyes went dark and sad, and she pulled her hand away, gripping it with the other. ''She had an aunt show up two days ago. The aunt wants Christina to come live with her.''

''Is that bad?''

Lacey's head lifted from her perusal of her hands. ''I think she just wants the money the state would pay her. Christina doesn't like her.''

''So how do you deal with that?''

''I need to find some way to prove she's not a good guardian for Christina.'' Her eyes were fierce. ''I'm going to figure out how to do that.''

''Want some help?''

Lacey's head whipped around. ''You would do that? Is it hard? I'm still pretty new at this.''

Dev snapped his fingers. ''Piece of cake. You just say the word.''

''I don't care what it costs. I just keep remembering how scared Christina was when I met her and how shaky she is still. She's so sweet, Dev, and she needs someone to love her—really love her for who she is inside.''

He thought Lacey's wish for Christina might mirror a wish of her own. There was a very big heart inside that slender frame. Dev would have given a lot to have someone fight for him like that.

"I work cheap for my friends. And tonight I'm running a special. You only need to agree to have dinner with me."

Lacey's mouth quirked. "I already agreed to that."

"Lucky you. You get off really cheap."

Her silvery eyes glowed. "We'll talk money later. I'm not letting you work for free."

"You don't have any choice. You ready?"

"For what?"

"Dinner."

Lacey looked around her at the darkened street. "Where are we going?"

He gestured to the stone building in front of them. "Right here."

Lacey couldn't help gaping. "Here? Dev, it's a museum. It's closed."

He smiled that cocky smile she'd seen so many times years ago. "Not to me. In my business, who you know is everything." He got out of the car and came around to help her alight. "This way, milady. The evening begins."

She felt a bubble of laughter rise in her throat. "Why is it, Devlin Marlowe, that you've always dared more than anyone else I've ever met?"

He tucked her hand under his elbow and looked down at her, his eyes hot and mysterious, his voice husky. "When the prize is worth it, a man will dare a lot."

Am I worth it, Dev? Her heart fluttered, but she didn't ask as Dev drew her forward.

The door opened as if by magic. "Good evening, Mr. Marlowe. Everything's in place." The security guard's tone was respectful. He tipped his hat to Lacey. "Evening, ma'am."

Lacey could barely get out a greeting, her mind whirling with wonder. "What have you done, Dev?"

He merely grinned. "You'll see."

He led her past paintings and sculptures, and she realized that he was leading her toward the courtyard. Anticipation bubbled like champagne in her blood.

The glow didn't register at first, but when it did, Lacey gasped in shock and went stock-still.

And then sighed.

The courtyard was alive with candlelight. There must have been hundreds of them placed strategically to create one island of light in the lushest corner of this space. Some were fat candles set in torches, some tapers in hurricane glass. Dozens more floated in the still fountain nearby.

Several tall urns were filled with long-stemmed roses allowed to open enough to share their fragrance, perfuming the night around them.

"Dev—" She pressed her hand to her breast, but she couldn't find the words.

His hand slid around her waist. "Do you like it?"

She heard the tiniest edge of nerves in his voice and turned to face him. "I've never seen anything this beautiful in my life."

"I have." He gazed at her, his eyes glowing as much from within as from the candlelight around them. He lifted his free hand to her chin and leaned toward her. "I'm looking at her now."

And then he brushed one soft kiss over her lips, tracing the moisture left behind with the pad of his thumb.

Lacey's heart was racing. "Oh, Dev—" She lifted slightly toward him, wanting more.

But he pulled away, his look regretful. He cleared his throat. "We might have an audience, I'm afraid. My connections don't extend far enough for them to abandon the place to us." He pressed one finger against her lips. "But hold that thought. I'm sure as hell going to."

The slight edge of disgruntlement in his tone made her want to giggle. She needed something, anything, to cool her own rapidly heating blood.

Dev led her forward, seating her on thick, fluffy jewel-tone cushions lying on top of a Persian rug sprinkled with ruby-red rose petals. Arrayed before them was a bucket of champagne and a spread she couldn't possibly eat, as the butterflies in her stomach were dodging the needle-sharp teeth of desire.

But somehow she did it, helped by Dev taking a position across from her, carefully out of reach. His physical presence was so powerful, she needed all the distance she could get.

It only helped a little. The soft weave of his slacks did not disguise his long, muscular legs, nor could his shirt adequately hide the breadth of his shoulders or the strength of his arms. Watching his long well-formed fingers wrapped around his flute of champagne made something deep and low in her burn.

Those hands had been on her once in complete abandon.

She wanted them on her again.

"How's the champagne?" he asked, but in his voice, she heard a darker shading that had her pulse kicking up.

Lacey made herself meet his gaze and wanted to sigh.

Dev was not classically handsome, but he was so magnetic, so undeniably male, so comfortable inside his skin that she envied him almost as much as she wanted to sigh like a teenage girl.

The teenage Lacey had been overwhelmed by Devlin Marlowe. The woman she was now was barely more able to keep from melting into a puddle.

"Lacey?" he prompted.

"What? Oh, yes—the champagne. It's good, Dev." Though she'd scarcely registered the slightest taste.

He filled in where her social skills failed her. Somehow, he turned the conversation to cases he'd had, amusing anecdotes about clients. Soon he had her laughing and forgetting that she was nervous.

Forgetting that she wanted his hands on her, though—well, even Dev wasn't a miracle worker.

They teased and talked and laughed for at least an hour, then finally Dev sat up from where he'd reclined on pillows like a pasha and reached for something behind him.

"All right. The pièce de résistance—" His French accent wasn't bad at all. With flair, he crossed the small space between them and opened a basket lined with satin.

Dark ovals lay inside, glowing in the candlelight. The scent was straight from heaven.

Lacey inhaled it like oxygen in a vacuum.

Dev set the lid down and plucked one oval from the basket, holding it above her lips. "Somewhere I got the idea that you're fond of chocolate."

Lacey grinned in memory. "I love chocolate, the darker the better."

Dev watched her mouth form the words and felt them right down to his groin. Stifling a groan of pure pain, he continued to tease her lush lips, wondering who he was actually torturing.

Her lips parted slightly in anticipation, and it was all Dev could do to recall that they were not alone.

He touched her lips lightly with the oval of dark chocolate, sliding it over that full lower lip of a mouth that ought to be against the law, then trailing it over the upper lip slowly.

Lacey's pink tongue lapped out, tracing the chocolate—and his fingers.

Dev did groan aloud then.

And cursed himself for a twice-damned fool.

With mingled mischief and heat in her eyes, Lacey licked out and sucked it from between his fingers, her warm, wet tongue scalding his skin. Dev dropped the basket to the rug and jerked her close, holding her head imprisoned as he sought surcease from her mouth.

She tasted of chocolate and champagne and sin. Dev's mind roared white-hot without a thought of where they were or who they were—just edgy, dark need wind-whipping his control into shreds.

Lacey rose to her knees and pressed herself

against him, her whimpers sounding as lost as he felt.

He had to have her. Had to be inside her at last. Too many years had gone by, but they were as nothing now. He was a man full-grown, with a man's needs, but he was also a lovesick young boy who only cared that a foretaste of heaven lay in his arms under moonlight's glow.

A siren screamed through the street outside and dimly penetrated the buzz in Dev's brain. He shook it off and shifted to slant his mouth against hers to go deeper, to reach for something that only Lacey could provide.

But the sound had registered on Lacey and she stiffened slightly, sighing against his lips.

Dev forced himself away, his chest heaving. He shoved to his feet before he took her right there, heedless of any audience. Need clawed at his chest and made him angry and uncaring of any cost he might bear.

But the strength of that very need reminded him that the barbarian in him was never far from the surface—and Lacey was a lady.

He risked a glance at her, seeing swollen lips and night-dark eyes, nerves skittering past the heaving breath of desire. He held out his hand. "I won't apologize for that."

Placing her hand in his, she looked up, humor scampering past nerves. "I won't ask you to."

That touch of humor shot down his spine worse than a blatant statement of desire ever could. "Damn. You're killing me. But I've got something else planned first."

"Really?" She smiled, her eyes lighting up as he helped her rise. "More?"

Her pleasure was more seductive than a hundred naked women parading past his view. He wanted to delight her, to challenge her notion of him, to show her that he was more than just a boy from the wrong side of the tracks, the one who hadn't been good enough for a princess to risk.

So he nodded and drew her toward the door. "More."

"Dev?" She dragged her feet behind him.

He turned, hope fading in his chest.

But those witchy silvery eyes were glowing. "Can we take the chocolate with us?"

Dev chuckled and returned for the basket. "You got it, babe." He returned to her side and glanced at her shoes. "Those things comfortable?"

Surprised, she glanced down. "Pretty much."

"Good." He led her back through the museum. "Why?"

"'Cause we're going dancin', darlin'."

"Dancing?" She sounded thrilled.

He nodded. "From the sublime—" he gestured at the artwork on the walls around them "—to the Supremes. We're going to take in the music of our youth."

She giggled. "Dev, those were the sixties. We were babies."

He quirked a grin. "Yeah, but I refuse to claim disco. I stake my turf in Motown. So come on, get moving, girl—those shoes are going to pay their dues."

She couldn't match his long strides, so he picked

her up in his arms, handing her the basket of chocolates. She popped one in her mouth and moaned like pure sex just as the security guard appeared.

The guard's grin was a mile wide. "You two have fun now." His gaze traveled down Lacey's long, slender legs, and his face turned wistful.

Dev shot him a warning glance, then grinned smugly. The best girl was his—at least for the night. "We plan to."

Then they were through the door and out on the sidewalk. Reaching the car, Dev slid her over the side without opening the door. Lacey reached up and popped a chocolate in his mouth, then rose to her knees on the seat and licked his lips, her breath sweet and dark.

Dev gripped her shoulders and eased her away from him before they got arrested for public lewdness. Violent need hummed beneath his skin, and he couldn't be responsible for the consequences if he answered that kiss.

Her sparking eyes told him she knew that.

"You, Ms. DeMille, are no lady, I'm beginning to think."

"Really?"

"You could sound a little more disgruntled."

Lacey grinned. "I don't want to be a lady tonight, Dev. I've been a lady too long." Her eyes taunted him.

The air went electric around them. Dev sucked in a ragged breath. "You are going to be in big trouble if you don't quit looking at me like that."

"Really?" She sounded more thrilled than ever.

Dev groaned aloud as he got in and started the car.

"Dev?"

"What?" He gritted his teeth, wondering why the devil he didn't just take her home and do what they were both craving.

Then he remembered that they were only on this magic island for a few hours. Then he would have to tell her.

If he were any kind of man, he'd take her home and tell her now.

But you owe us this, he snarled at the heavens. *Our one magic night was stolen from us, and this is the only one we might ever get.*

He hoped he was wrong. That maybe, just maybe, it would be enough to give them a fighting chance. He knew now that he wanted that chance more than he'd ever wanted anything in his life.

"You okay?" she asked.

"Hmm?" Dev shook off his torment, realizing she'd said something he hadn't heard. He forced his thoughts to lighten. "Oh, sorry. Yeah, I'm fine." He gripped her hand probably a little too tightly, pressing a hot, wet kiss to her knuckles.

"So, Devlin Marlowe, you haven't answered my question." But her voice was just the tiniest bit shaky.

"What question?"

"Are you going to teach me how to jitterbug?"

Dev shot her a look, drinking in the delight fracturing the shadows in her eyes.

They deserved this night, and he was going to see that they got it.

"Yeah," he answered, his voice rough. "I'm going to show you a lot of things you never saw before."

Some of them even while we're still dressed.

The Caddy shot through the night.

Chapter Nine

Lacey had no idea where they were heading. They'd long ago left any part of town she'd ever seen.

"Don't be scared. I promise it's not as bad as it looks," Dev said, his voice tight.

She touched his arm gently. "I'm not afraid. I'm with you."

He muttered under his breath, something about the wrong side of the tracks. "You don't belong here. This is a bad idea."

"Dev—" She touched his hand. "I loved Shorty's doughnuts, didn't I? Stop treating me like I'm made of glass."

She saw the tension in his jaw ease slightly.

"If you don't like it, we don't have to stay."

"And if I do?"

He glanced at her. "It's not your kind of place, Lacey. I don't know what I was thinking. You belong in someplace with piano music."

"Stop it, Dev. I want to be someone new."

An odd look crossed his face at those words.

"I mean it." She spread her arms wide, throwing her head back and wishing her hair were long so it could whip in the wind like a banner.

"If you don't stop looking like seven kinds of sin, I will not be responsible for my actions," he growled.

A slow, lazy smile spread across her lips. She arched one eyebrow. "Really?"

"And if you say 'really' one more time like you're licking your chops over forbidden thrills, I definitely won't be responsible."

She couldn't resist. "Really?" She threw back her head and laughed.

He slammed to a stop in a parking lot and jerked her against him, covering her mouth in a kiss so hot she was sure her lungs were scorched.

But Lacey didn't care. This was the best night of her whole life, and she was going to live it to the fullest. She'd never felt more alive, her nerve endings sizzling like severed high wires dancing on the ground in a shower of sparks.

Dev took her under again, and she thought she'd lost the ability to breathe...but she didn't care. Giddy laughter bubbled up her throat, and she wanted to sing and shout and dance.

He pulled away slightly; she gripped his hair in her hands and nibbled at his lower lip. "Don't stop."

Was that her voice, so low and hungry?

"I have to, or we're not making it out of this car." Dev sounded a little breathless, and Lacey was inordinately pleased to think she could have that effect on him.

"Am I a femme fatale, Dev?" she asked innocently.

Dev growled low in his throat. "You are pure hell-born trouble. I'm shocked at you." But he was grinning even as his eyes sparked with something dark and dangerous.

She inhaled to speak.

"Do not say 'really'—"

Lacey laughed. She'd only had one glass of champagne but she felt like she could fly. "Take me dancing, Dev." Her voice lowered. "And then take me home."

His nostrils flared. "When I do, I'm going to want to stay," he warned.

She licked her lips, loving the way he sucked in a breath as he watched her. "I hope so."

Dev cursed under his breath and broke from the car like demons were after him. He stood outside with his hands on the door, his knuckles white. "Don't tease me, Lacey. Not about this." Suddenly his eyes were that boy's eyes, almost pleading.

She crawled over his seat and emerged from the car, settling her hands on his. "Never about this, Dev." She took a deep breath. "Never."

Dev shut the car door and grasped her hand, pulling her into his side. "If I last one dance, it'll be a miracle." He sounded thoroughly disgruntled, and Lacey giggled.

But he lasted a lot more than one dance. The place could only politely be called a dive, but Lacey had more fun than she'd had at any expensive society function. They didn't talk much—the music was too loud for that. But it was great music, fast and full of energy and fun.

Dev taught her dances whose names she couldn't possibly remember, but she didn't care. He was a superb dancer, gliding and whirling her around the floor with muscular grace. He even did something she'd wanted to do all her life—have her partner slide her between his legs, then lift her over his head as they jitterbugged like crazy.

She was sweaty and hot and out of breath when he declared a rest break. Gratefully, they sank into chairs as Dev ordered beers for both of them.

"Sorry." He shrugged. "No wine in this place."

She lifted the beer bottle to her lips and took several deep swallows.

Dev's eyebrows rose. "You like it?"

She shook her head. "It tastes terrible. But it's wet." And then she laughed and pulled his head toward hers, sinking into a beery kiss.

"I'm having so much fun, Dev," she murmured. "Thank you for this."

She saw him swallow before he answered, staring at his beer bottle and picking at the label. "This is who I am, Lacey. I've got money now, and I make a good living. But losing everything when my dad died taught me that none of that is important." He lifted his bottle for another swallow, but paused. "You have to know that about me. I don't want your money. I don't like it, or what it makes people think about who they are compared to others.'' He tipped the bottle back, his strong throat moving with each swallow.

Lacey's mouth went dry with lust, but she was more shaken than she could say by his words. ''Is that what you think of me, Dev? That I'm like them?''

He set the bottle down and slanted her a glance. ''I used to.'' He exhaled. ''I don't want to, now.''

Lacey covered his hand with hers, the long, strong fingers so beautiful to her that they made her want to weep. ''Don't,'' she whispered. ''See me as me.''

Dev curled his fingers around hers. ''You want to go?''

Lacey nodded. ''If you do.'' Her heart set up a tip-tap beat, thinking of what might happen next.

Then Dev drew to attention, as if scenting the wind. The band had begun the first few notes of a slow song. He turned back to her. ''We can't leave yet. This is my favorite song in the whole wide world.'' He drew her onto the dance floor again, and into his arms.

Then Lacey recognized it, and whatever was left of her heart tumbled at Dev's feet. ''My Girl,'' the song by the Temptations that had made millions of women swoon.

Lacey swayed in Dev's arms, held close and safe as he moved them gracefully across the floor, humming the words in her ear. Her throat filled with something that felt a lot like tears.

They should have been dancing to this song for the last seventeen years. They should have been making love and having babies and holding each other in the night.

Lacey burrowed into Dev's chest and wanted to weep for all the lost years, for all that had been taken from them on that dark, terrible night. She should have stood up for him, should have seen the man he would become. If she had, maybe he would never have been forced into that fateful decision, but she knew now that whatever his reason, she would give him a fair audience because she had played a part in all of it. If she had been up-front with her father and not sneaked around with Dev, perhaps her parents would have accepted him. Perhaps they could have—

"Shh," Dev murmured, his voice smoky and low. With his fingers, he dried her tears. "Don't think about the past, Lacey." It was as if he had read her thoughts. "Think about now...tonight." He lowered his head. "Think about this."

Then Dev covered her mouth with a kiss of such poignant sweetness that her heart felt as though it would explode from the press of all she wanted to say to him.

He pulled back slightly. "This is our song now. And tonight is our night." He brushed her lips with his thumb. "Let me take you home, Lacey. Let me love you tonight. Whatever else happens, we deserve this much."

In his voice she heard a note of foreboding, and she wanted to tell him that nothing outside them would ever matter again. She would not let it.

But his eyes pleaded for a ceasefire from the past. So Lacey merely nodded, lifting to her tiptoes and giving him back a soft kiss. "Please, Dev. Take me home. I want the night we should have had."

She saw a shiver ripple up his spine and felt a rush of gratitude that she could affect him so deeply.

Tonight is ours, Dev. But I want more.

But it was too soon to say such a thing, so Lacey merely smiled and rested her head against his chest.

Dev pulled her tightly under his arm and headed for the car.

The ride to her town house was silent, but the silence was charged with layers of emotion—the low hum of intense need, the poignancy of so many years lost, the newly discovered comfort of each other's presence. Dev held Lacey's hand the entire way, thinking about how he never wanted to let her go.

Please, he pleaded, hoping that somewhere someone was listening. *Make this enough to shield her from hurt. Don't let me be part of the pain. Let me be her comfort, not her tormentor.*

He didn't want to tell her wrong. He wanted to handle everything right so that she could see the richness of having two families to love her.

Maddie had enough love in her for the whole world. Mitch and Boone would give her strength.

But Dev wanted to steal Lacey away from all of this, to keep her for himself, to make himself her guardian from all harm.

You're an ice-cold witch, he told Fate. *After all these years, after I thought I'd gotten over her, tried to forget that she even existed, you bring her back*

*into my life and you make me the instrument of the
toughest shift she'll ever have to weather.*

Damn you, Dev thought. Fate had pulled another
fast one on Devlin Marlowe. But it was himself he
damned as he pulled into Lacey's driveway. It was
the gentle creature beside him who would bear the
brunt if he didn't do this right.

He shut off the car, at war with himself over
whether or not to say it now, get it over with.

Lacey took the decision out of his hands, sliding
across the seat and wrapping her arms around his
neck. Her silvery eyes glowed in the moonlight.
"Thank you, Dev," she whispered. "This is the
best night of my entire life."

Then she pressed her lips to his, and all the emotion that was inside Dev rushed like a river, swamp-
ing his brain.

I've been waiting for you, he thought in amaze-
ment. *All my life…and it was you, all along.*

The time for words was past. Dev gentled the
kiss, pulling away with real regret. He opened his
door and swept Lacey up in his arms, kicking the
car door closed and striding to her door.

Once inside, he headed with sure steps to her
bedroom, remembering the night that he'd sat outside, wondering if she was dreaming of him, knowing she would keep robbing him of sleep until they
could settle what was between them.

If it was a battle, Lacey had won, taking no pris-
oners. That she'd turned her back on the boy mattered nothing to the man who understood now that
life threw you a lot of curveballs, but life was what
you made it.

She'd been so young, so protected. If he had a bone to pick, it was now and forever with Charles DeMille.

And as Dev settled Lacey on pale lavender silk, the last thing he wanted to think about was Lacey's father.

Her filmy skirt settled around the legs that haunted his dreams, tucked up to display one pale, smooth thigh. Dev felt a bolt of longing, sharp and painful. Her eyes were huge and dark as moonlight silvered across her bed.

Just as they'd been on that night so long ago.

"It should have been you, Dev." Her voice was throaty and low. "I wanted you to be the first."

The ache in her eyes nearly undid him.

"Shh," he whispered, pressing one finger over her lips. "I'm here now." He placed one knee on the bed beside her waist, leaning on arms suddenly gone weak.

"Dev?" Her breath wafted warm across his temple as he lowered his head to the pulse in her throat.

She grasped his head when he didn't answer. "You need to know that except for one big mistake, there's hardly been anyone. I didn't want—" She cut her gaze away, then back. "None of them were you."

Dev squeezed his eyes shut. "Lacey, if you want me to last, don't tell me things like that."

She gripped his head in her hands and forced him to face her. "I don't," she said fiercely. "I want you inside me. Now. I've wondered a thousand times how it would have felt—knowing that it was you, Dev—always your touch I should have known first.''

Seized by a gut-deep need that sliced like a thousand knives, Dev lowered his head to hers and took her mouth, no holds barred.

Lacey whimpered but answered with a hunger of her own, a hunger so strong he could feel it vibrating her bones. She gripped his hair in her fingers and pressed her body upward.

Dear heaven. He was half-blind with need. When her fingers tore at his shirt, his own were there, too.

Lacey shoved his shirt off his shoulders and ran her fingers over his chest, sliding them through the dark hair and digging her nails lightly into his skin.

Dev's mind arced white with longing. With fingers turned clumsy, he tried to find the opening of her dress while Lacey's own hands descended to his belt buckle.

''How the hell,'' he muttered, ''do you undo this damn dress?''

A slight smile ghosted over Lacey's taut features. ''Side—'' she gasped, unbuckling his belt and reaching for the clasp of his slacks ''—zipper.''

Dev grabbed her wrists firmly. Chest heaving, he sucked in a breath, staring down into desire-drenched eyes. ''Lacey, slow down. This is too important.'' He settled her hands down by her sides and clasped her cheek. ''I don't want to rush.''

Lacey's smile was wicked. ''We have all night, Dev. We can take it slow next time.''

''No.'' *We might not have a next time.* Then he settled for what he could tell her of the truth right now. ''I never expected this.'' He glanced away, running one hand through his hair. Then he looked back. "I never thought I'd see you again, not after—"

Her eyes went dark and sad. "I don't know why you did it, Dev, but it doesn't matter anymore. We're here tonight, and that's enough."

"Why I did what?" Dev frowned.

She shook her head. "There's no reason to discuss it. It's over."

"What's over? What is it you think I've done?" Unease crawled up his spine.

She looked so uncomfortable. "Don't. We don't have to talk about it."

"Lacey," he warned, grasping her hands. "I need to know what you're talking about. Are you referring to that night?" He knew he didn't have to specify which one.

Tears shimmered in her eyes. "Daddy told me what you did, and I didn't want to believe it at first, but then you never tried to contact me again, so I knew it must be true." She looked away from him for a second, then her gaze returned to his. "It hurt so badly, Dev." She swallowed hard. "But we were young. I don't need to know why."

Dev slid his hands up to her shoulders, his voice going hard. "Tell me what you think I did." Inside him, a beast was stirring, a dark being of haunted shadows and hateful proportions.

"It's okay. I understand. You were poor. I just wish you'd—" Her voice broke, and tears spilled past her lashes.

The boy inside him ached. "I wanted to talk to you. I wanted to write you, but he made me prom-

ise. I had to leave the next morning and stay away
for good or my family would suffer. They'd already
lost too much. I couldn't bring them more pain.''
His jaw clenched so hard he could almost feel teeth
crack. "I wanted to—but I couldn't. And you had
walked away without a backward glance. I didn't
think you'd care.''

Heartbreak filled her eyes. "I wrote you letter
after letter from school in Switzerland. I sent them
to your mother's house. I wanted to understand why
you did it, but you never answered.''

"I never got any letters, Lacey." He saw her
eyes widen, then her brow furrowed. Dev's stomach
clenched. "What did he tell you I did?''

Unease fled across her face. She dropped her
gaze and whispered. "You wanted money to walk
away. It hurt so badly to know that, but I think I
understand—''

The breath whooshed out of her as Dev gripped
her shoulders and lifted her off the bed. "He told
you I took *money?*" Rage roared through his veins.
"He threatened me with jail, Lacey. He knew I
wouldn't take his money—I was working for him
as little better than a slave because I refused to take
one damn dime from him that I didn't earn. He
made my family into a charity case and he never
missed an opportunity to rub it in my face that I
couldn't take care of them properly myself.''

"You're hurting me, Dev." Her eyes were wide
and dark, her face pale as water.

He let go instantly, jerking back and rubbing his
hands over his face. "I'm sorry. God, I'm sorry—''
He leaped from the bed and began to pace.

"I want to believe you," she said in a tiny voice.

He whirled. "What?"

Lacey sat up, hands rubbing her upper arms. "I said, I want to believe you." She looked up at him, stricken. "But why would he do that?"

"Because—" Dev's laugh was bitter "—as he said, I wasn't good enough for his princess." He clawed one hand through his hair, then exhaled sharply and went to kneel at her side.

"I'm sorry. I'm so sorry I held you too roughly. I wouldn't hurt you for anything in the world."

It was true. The last thing he wanted to do was to hurt her. Dev wanted to shake his fists at the heavens. Instead, he stared at the floor, shoulders hunched in defeat. Would she feel better or worse to know that the man who had done that to them wasn't her blood father?

He felt a touch on his hair so gentle he could have imagined it. "He was wrong," she whispered. "You're special. You've always been special."

And she slid her slender hands to frame his face, tipping it up to the moonlight where he could see the gentle outpouring of something that made his heart seize. Almost reverently, she lowered her mouth to his, pausing less than a breath away.

"Don't let him win," she whispered. "Come back to this bed and make love to me."

If he could have handed her the world in that moment, he would have done it. With fingers that weren't quite steady, he touched her hair as gently as a baby's breath. Lacey's lips brushed his, and the moment felt holy.

Dev let her set the pace, and when she deepened

the kiss, he fought to hold back the outpouring of years of longing, of the unshed tears of a boy who'd been too bad, too poor, too young to become a man soon enough to keep those he loved from suffering.

Lacey's kiss was both balm and torture. He pulled her off the bed and onto his lap, closing her into his arms and wishing he could hold off the world.

He drank in the succor like a man long in the desert, but even as he felt years of pain ease, his heart squeezed.

I don't want to tell you. I don't want to hurt you.

But he had to tell her. With everything in him, he prayed he would do it right. Find the magic words to deliver the news without tearing her apart.

Then the sweetness couldn't hold the fire at bay any longer. In seconds more, he could feel the lick of flames at his heels, hear the roaring of the inferno racing toward them.

She whimpered and squirmed in his arms. Dev bent over her to shelter her from harm and took them deeper into the bliss.

It was everything, Lacey thought. This. This man. Dev, it was Dev she had waited for, Dev who'd been the reason that no one else was ever enough. Only Dev could ease the gnawing ache, fill the emptiness that had been her constant companion for years.

With that dawning of understanding, something inside her eased open like a flower in the light. Dev was her dark sun, her other half, the man who could finally make her whole.

And now Lacey burned, the long night of teasing

and sweet torture scraping her nerve endings to
screaming attention. Sliding her nails over his skin,
she nipped at his lips, sought his tongue, pressed
herself close enough that their skin could meld, become one.

And Dev answered her with a power that flared
through her like a star burst. His strong arms held
her so close she could barely breathe, but she
couldn't care less. She wanted to be closer still.

"Dev," she demanded, helpless against how he
made her feel. "Now. Please...now."

His fingers worked her zipper, then he slipped
the halter strap over her head, sliding his hands
down the open bodice and baring her breasts to his
view.

Lacey had never felt more naked in her life,
though she was only bare from the waist up. She
lifted her hands to cover herself, but Dev grasped
her wrists.

"No," he said, his voice rough and low. Then
he bent and took one nipple in his mouth.

Lacey cried out, arching backward, hoping Dev
would catch her as ecstasy arrowed through every
nerve.

He did, clasping her in his strong arms, holding
her just loosely enough to give him access.

She squirmed in his lap, wanting to get closer,
digging her fingers in his thick dark hair and pressing his head closer.

Dev chuckled and trailed a long, slow, wet kiss
across the valley to her other breast.

When his tongue circled the curve, Lacey
groaned.

"I can't stand it," she whispered harshly.

He paused long enough to slant the devil's own green eyes at her, smiling. "Yes, you can." Then his eyes darkened and he covered her mouth with his own, kissing her as though she held the key to his survival.

He gathered her up and rose as though she weighed nothing, never breaking the hot, deep kiss that was melting her from the inside out. Sliding his hands beneath her, he lifted her dress, then sat her on the bed and pulled the garment over her head.

Dev parted her legs and knelt between them, sliding her shoes off with his warm hands, then cradling each foot as though it were precious.

Slowly trailing his fingers up her calves, he bent and kissed the inside of one knee with a long, hot, wet slide of his tongue that continued up her thigh.

Lacey sucked in a breath against the sheer glory of it, squeezing her legs around his chest.

Then Dev lifted his head, his eyes almost black with longing. His warm hands gripped her thighs up high, his thumbs stroking nearer and nearer as he gazed into her eyes with a sadness that made her want to cry.

"Forget before," she whispered. "This is the only time that matters. This is our first."

"Lacey—" He stopped, his hands squeezing. "I should tell you—"

"Shh, not now—whatever it is can wait." She lay back on the covers, sliding her fingers over his hair. "Come to me, Dev. Make me yours. This is the night that was stolen from us."

She slid her fingers beneath the elastic of her panties, ready to remove them.

Eyes burning, Dev stopped her with his hands, imprisoning her fingers as he placed his mouth over the silk and blew hot breath over the most intimate part of her.

She gasped. Goose bumps skipped all over her body. He rose and stepped back, those long, strong fingers sliding the panties away. Lacey watched as he stepped out of his shoes, removed his socks, then unfastened his slacks and slid them off. She bit her lower lip as she saw Dev's body revealed to her for the first time.

"You're beautiful," she whispered. And he was, fiercely beautiful in the way of a warrior's body. Dark hair curled on his chest, tapering down his flat belly and disappearing inside his briefs. His legs were long and well-made, his shoulders broad, his arms muscular. He made her toes curl with longing.

Dev slipped his thumbs inside the waistband of his briefs, and Lacey rose quickly. "Let me." Was that her voice, so husky?

He was so hard, so ready. As though she was unwrapping the best Christmas present of her life, Lacey slid her fingers beneath the band where his eager body strained the elastic. She heard Dev suck in a breath when he realized what she was doing.

Swirling one slow lick over his manhood, Lacey savored the taste and the texture of him. She slid the briefs down farther and took him in her mouth.

Dev's fingers tightened in her hair, and he groaned. "Wait—Lacey, wait." He tried to pull her head back, but she slid her tongue down the shaft.

"Let me have you," he growled, pushing her head away. "I have to have you, Lacey. Don't do this."

She lifted her head and smiled.

Dev growled and gently lifted her onto her back, kicking off his briefs and following her down to the bed, sealing her mouth in a kiss so scorching that she felt it to the soles of her feet.

Dev thought his heart would stop as her legs parted beneath him and she edged the heat of her against the part of him that was screaming for relief. He wanted to be inside her so badly he thought his heart would explode.

"It was you who taught me what passion was, Dev. Finish the lesson. Make me the woman I should have been long ago."

Dev kissed her with all the longings that had been bottled up for years. "You're the one, Lacey," he whispered. "The only one." He held her face in his hands like a promise he wanted badly to keep. "Look at me, sweetheart."

She opened those witchy silver eyes, the pupils huge and dark, and she was so open to him that he felt his heart tear. "Mine," he vowed. "Then and now." And with one smooth thrust, he joined them.

They both went still in a hushed, silent moment where past pain was annealed by the present.

Tears slid into Lacey's hair. "So long," she whispered. "I've waited for you so long, Dev."

A shiver rippled over her skin, and he felt it move over his heart. And then he let the madness take them, desperate to bind her to him, to make up for so many years of being without her. Stars burst behind his eyes and his chest burned with the force of all the words he couldn't yet say, the memories that pounded his heart.

She should have been mine, was all he could think. *All this time, she should have been mine.*

His eyes were damp. He pulled her closer, drove deeper, desperate to remove the barrier of skin, to make them one body. One heart. One soul.

And through his thoughts threaded a prayer. *Please. Don't take her from me again.*

Then the stars went nova—and sent them soaring into uncharted space.

Chapter Ten

Dev sped through the streets as dawn pearled the sky. Everything in him wished that he hadn't checked his voice mail when he'd been unable to sleep, filled with dread. Waiting for Lacey to wake up so he could do what he could no longer put off—tell her about her past.

He wanted to be back in that bed with Lacey, savoring the fire and sweetness between them. Instead, he was on his way to his brother's after Connor's urgent message.

This had damn well better be life or death, buddy. His brother, who could sleep through a nuclear blast, who never got up before noon on Saturday, had been awake when he'd returned the call—and agitated. He insisted that Dev come to see him, said he could not discuss the matter on the

phone. Dev had left Lacey a note, but he hoped to
be back before she woke. He'd wanted to kiss her,
but if she awoke when he did…well, he already
knew where that would lead.

So sweet and hot, that slender body. So rich and
open, that gentle heart. Dev had imagined making
love to Lacey a thousand times since that long-ago
night, but his imagination had been far too puny.
They'd made love all through a magical, star-
drenched night. He wanted to stay in that magic
forever.

But he still had news to deliver. Dev raked anxious fingers through his hair. The ante had just gone
up because now he didn't kid himself that he'd be
able to walk away whole if she despised him for
being the messenger.

Too many years had gone by, and all of them a
wasteland. After last night, he realized he'd been
starving to death. Lost in the desert and parched
down to his soul.

Lacey was it. The one. He'd been waiting for her
all his life. What he'd told himself for all these
years was complete self-deception.

Everything in him longed to turn around and
climb back in that bed, pull her into his arms and
hold on tight. But chances were far more likely that
she'd never want to speak to him again once he'd
done his duty.

He slammed the car to a stop outside Connor's
and emerged, grim and determined. He'd get Connor settled, whatever this was about, then go back
to Lacey and try his damnedest not to screw up this

miracle that he didn't deserve—but would fight to keep.

Connor pulled open the door, ushered him inside.

"You look like ten kinds of hell. What's going on?" Dev asked. "Are you in trouble, Connor?"

"No." His brother frowned at the insult. "It's not about me. It's about Dad."

"What about him?"

Connor fell silent, his face troubled.

"I came here instead of going back to a bed I didn't want to leave, bud. Spit it out."

Connor exhaled sharply. "Dad was framed."

"What?" But though the words rocked him, Dev knew how much he wanted it to be true. The man he remembered would never have— "Innocent," Dev said grimly. "He was innocent all along."

"No—not innocent, not from what I can tell here. He cooked the books, there's no question about that. He kept his working papers."

Dev felt sick. "So what are you telling me?"

"He did it at someone's direction. He left notes to cover himself."

"Why?" Dev couldn't square it. "Why would he do it, even if someone asked?"

"It was a bad time, Dev. We studied it in school. The mid-eighties in Texas were tough all over, but the problems started earlier in Houston with an oil bust. Businesses were going under by the hundreds. Big accounting firms were laying off people right and left. Dad had four kids."

And a wife with expensive tastes, Dev thought. Connor was too young to remember the trips, the jewelry, the big house. "Whose direction?" But his gut was already starting to twinge.

"The firm's biggest account needed financing to keep them afloat. The real books couldn't survive a lender's scrutiny. DeMille and Marshall couldn't afford to lose the account. Dad made the fraudulent entries. The client got the loan. Everything was fine until the Securities and Exchange Commission did an audit. Dad took the fall."

"Who, Connor? Dad wouldn't have done that on his own. Who made him sign the working papers?"

But his gut already knew before Connor said the words.

"The senior partner. Charles DeMille."

Dev squeezed his eyes shut against the roaring in his brain. Finally, it all fit. The unusual interest of Charles DeMille in their family's plight. The false solicitousness of a man who had even more to lose than Patrick Marlowe had.

His charity took on a whole new light. It was hush money, paid just in case anything had been left behind.

"He might as well have put a gun to Dad's head. He killed him just as surely as if he'd pulled the trigger." Dev started pacing. He wanted to smash something, wanted to tear out Charles DeMille's throat.

You're nothing. You never were.

That bastard. Dev could still see the terror on Lacey's face from that long-ago night. Still feel the shame of being cast out for being not good enough for his princess.

The princess who was never DeMille's blood at all. Lies. Lies upon lies.

"Dev? You all right?"

Dev looked at his watch. Six-thirty. A little early to go calling, but who the hell cared?

"Will those papers hold up in court, Connor?"

"They'll raise enough questions to force the issue. I'm no lawyer, but I'd think they'd certainly convince a judge to subpoena records."

"Keep them safe. Don't say anything to Mom or the girls, all right?" Dev's head began to pound.

"What are you going to do?"

"He took our father away from us. He took our name. He took everything—" Dev's jaw clenched. His eyes were hard as he stared into the past. "I'm going to return the favor. Show me. Show me what you've got. Every detail."

"You want to get some sleep first? Where have you been?"

With the daughter of the man who ruined us. Dev stifled a harsh laugh and ignored Connor's question. "Sleep is the last thing on my mind." Dev forced himself to exhale slowly, get the churning in his stomach under control. "Show me."

He followed Connor to the dining table where papers were spread out all over everywhere. "Just to think that all this time, it was sitting there, waiting for us." He cursed softly. "All these years, we could have—"

It didn't bear thinking. The sense of loss staggered him.

"What are you planning?" Connor asked. "I don't like the look on your face."

For a moment, Dev simply stared at the papers without picking them up, his thoughts careening from one stunning implication to another.

None of it had to happen. None of the pain.

His mother hadn't had to drink away the anguish. His siblings could have had a father. They hadn't had to be inches away from welfare.

You bastard. Charles DeMille's smug certainty flared in his face. *You lousy, arrogant liar.*

The scared fifteen-year-old boy hadn't had to lie awake at night in terror. The eighteen-year-old hadn't had to leave everyone who mattered.

I hope you burn in hell. I'm going to help you get there, Dev vowed.

"I'm going to pay a little early morning visit to River Oaks." He shook his head and reached for a stack of papers, his jaw grinding. "You got coffee made?"

Lacey woke up wanting him. Her body tingled with the sweet hum of arousal. He'd made love to her all through the night, each time tinged with a desperation that touched her to her soul. Intense, as though he needed to make up for long years lost apart. She'd felt the same need. They'd driven each other crazy with a hunger that grew with every touch, every caress, every greedy plundering. When she'd finally fallen into helpless slumber, the feel of his strong body wrapped around hers had given her the best few hours of sleep of her life.

She wanted him again. Now. Dev had unleashed something primal in her. A wanton creature she'd never met.

Lacey stretched her humming, hungry body. She was incredibly proud of herself. She'd been anything but a lady.

Lacey grinned. She'd been an animal last night.

Her mother would be scandalized.

Perfect.

Sunlight warmed her face as she felt the slight ache of muscle, the deep inner heat from greed given, need absorbed.

You hussy. Lacey smiled in delight. She'd never once woken up naked in her entire life. Naked and filled with a crackling energy that demanded attention.

She'd seduce him this morning. Take him. Show him a new face of the tigress he'd unleashed.

Ready to see if she could scandalize Dev, too, she rolled over to find him, to place her greedy hands on that hard, beautiful body that sent need swimming through her veins.

Her hand brushed sheets disappointingly cool to the touch. She opened her eyes to find the bed empty beside her.

Dev was gone.

A piece of paper was propped on the bedside table, her name scrawled on the outside in a bold hand.

Two rose petals lay in front of it, scarlet reminders of a night seared forever in her memory. She was smiling when she opened the note.

Lacey—

I'm sorry. I want to be there with you right now, but I have to go help my brother. Damn voice mail.

Stay warm. Stay naked. If you can't stay naked, keep your cell phone on. I'll find you. Don't forget where we left off.

Dev

Lacey pressed a kiss to the paper and set it on the table. Picking up the rose petals, she brushed them over her lips, inhaled the last traces of fragrance. Remembered a night that had been a dream. A revelation.

A fantasy they'd been denied for seventeen years.

Thanks to her father.

The morning's glow faded. How could he have done that? He'd always been very protective of her and yes, finding your daughter writhing naked in the gazebo had to be a shock.

But she'd always been so dutiful until then. Forbidding her would have been enough after that humiliation, much as she hated to admit it. Why lie? Why participate in breaking her heart? It had devastated her, believing that Dev had prized money over her. It had robbed her, stolen deep into her never-strong faith in her judgment. The disaster with Luc had been part and parcel of proving something to herself—and look how that had ended.

But her father had always loved her so fiercely. Surely he wouldn't have done it if he'd realized what it would take from her. How it would begin the fading of her belief in herself. He loved her. She was his princess.

She had to understand why he had done it. Had

to make it clear that he must stay out of this now. Whatever she and Dev could make of this magic, it was theirs. Between them. Her father might have thought he'd been acting in her best interests.

He'd been wrong. From now on, whatever he thought of Dev, this was her life. Her heart. Her future.

Rising from the bed, she padded toward the bathroom to get ready. Her father never left the house before nine on Saturdays. While Dev was gone, she would make a quick trip over there. Get answers, make her stand clear.

No more interference. It was time he remembered that she was a grown woman.

And time she acted like one.

"This had better be important, Devlin." Charles DeMille looked as arrogant as ever, spoke to him as before, man to boy. "Is this about Lacey? I thought you must be behind the breakup. You leave her alone."

But Dev wasn't a boy anymore. He faced his enemy with the assurance that he'd mastered everything life had thrown at him. Everything this man had started rolling.

To keep the upper hand, Dev remained silent, looking around him. He had never been allowed inside this house, but it looked very much as he would have expected. The library's rich, dark paneling was almost a cliché, reeking of money and sacrificed forests. The scent of forbidden Cuban cigars hovered in the air.

Finally, he spoke. "Lacey is not the issue right now."

"You stay away from my daughter. I told you once before, but you never listened, did you, Devlin?"

"Oh, I heard what you said." Every word came from between clenched teeth. Dev wanted to take this man's smug superiority and ram it down his throat. *I came from your daughter's bed,* he wanted to say, just to wipe that smugness off DeMille's face—but he didn't. It wasn't fair to Lacey.

"I haven't forgotten anything you've said—or done." Dev cocked an eyebrow and let silence spin out for a moment longer. Few people could stand silence; most would rush to fill it.

"Do you know what time it is?" DeMille demanded.

Dev nodded, still not speaking.

"Why are you here, Marlowe?"

Dev waited another long, pregnant pause. "Does the name Allied Drilling ring a bell?"

DeMille's color paled slightly, but he hadn't gotten his riches from being a pushover. He recovered quickly. "Doesn't ring a bell. What's this about?"

"Does the word fraud help your memory?"

Charles DeMille's body went rigid. "What are you trying to imply?"

"My father kept working papers. I'm going to take you down, DeMille. I'm going to disgrace you like you disgraced my father." Dev wanted to wade in with his fists. With immense effort, he kept his fingers loose, his hands at his sides. "You sanctimonious bastard. You set up my father to take the fall, then you rode to the rescue like some knight in shining armor. Had my mother singing your praises when all along, it was you who robbed us of everything.''

He walked closer, testing himself. How close could he get and not smash in the guy's face? ''You played the savior and all the while you knew—''

Dev had to swallow back the rage that was darkening his vision.

DeMille wasn't giving in. ''Your father made the entries in his own hand. You can't prove otherwise.'' He smiled. ''You can't afford to fight me, Devlin. I hire lawyers by the gross.''

''It will surprise you to know that I've done quite well for myself. I'm willing to spend every dime taking you down.''

DeMille's lip curled. ''You can't win. My name means something in this town. Yours is tainted.''

''I don't have to go to court to change that. I can ruin you without ever entering the courthouse.''

''You're using Lacey to get to me, aren't you?'' DeMille asked. ''This is all about me. You never got over getting caught with your pants down, being taken down to size in front of her.''

''Leave Lacey out of this.''

DeMille's eyes sharpened. ''You silly pup. She's still too good for you. She always will be. Don't go thinking you can have her now. You're still a mongrel, however well that mongrel is dressed.''

''I know about Lacey.''

DeMille frowned faintly. ''Know what?''

''Does the name Jenny Wallace ring a bell?''

DeMille's eyes widened. In them, Dev saw his revenge. Fear sparked there. Arrogance faltered.

"You can't prove a thing," DeMille bluffed.

"I can, and when she knows, it will be over. She'll never forgive you. You've lied to her all her life. You had the nerve to tell me that I wasn't good enough for your precious, blue-blooded daughter— and she isn't even your blood. You told me I was nothing—when it was you who made me that way. You who created the whole nightmare and then framed my father."

"I won't let you use Lacey to get to me. You can't prove anything."

"Are you going to tell her, or shall I, DeMille? She already knows that you—"

Voices outside the door broke into his consciousness. The voices of women—

Lacey's voice.

"What are you doing here at this hour, darling?" Her mother stood on the stairs in an immaculate satin robe.

"I need to talk to Daddy. Where is he?"

She looked at the elegant entry, at her mother standing so straight and dignified on the staircase. She remembered a thousand hours of her childhood, the pride in her father's voice, the hours she and her mother had spent together.

Surely there was an explanation.

"He's in the library. Darling, is something wrong?"

Lacey shook her head. "I need to speak to Daddy first."

Her mother frowned but continued her descent. "All right. But I don't know what could be so important at this unearthly hour."

Lacey followed her mother down the hallway. They both stopped for a moment at the sound of a very angry voice.

Dev's voice. She hadn't noticed his car outside.

"I won't let you use Lacey to get to me. You can't prove anything." Her father's voice was almost a shout.

"Are you going to tell her, or shall I, DeMille? She already knows that you—"

She glanced at her mother just as the door opened. Her father stood inside, looking years older.

Dev stood behind him, a stranger to her. His face was all hard, brutal angles. And shadows.

"What are you doing here, Lacey?" Dev's expression shifted to one of concern. "Go on back home," he said gently.

But she didn't like what she felt in the air. What she'd heard. Lacey glanced between the two men. "What's going on?"

She looked at Dev. "Is he going to tell me what?"

"Come sit down, princess." Her father settled her in one of the big leather wing chairs and hovered beside her. He looked anxious. Unsettled.

"I don't want to sit." She got to her feet.

"What's this about, Charles?" her mother asked.

"It's about the past, Mrs. DeMille," Dev responded.

Her mother's look at Dev was pure disdain. "Charles?"

"Lacey, has he harmed you?" Her father neared her side.

She surprised even herself by backing away from her father one step.

Hurt darkened his eyes. "Why have you come, princess?"

"I'd like to speak to my parents alone, please, Dev."

Dev didn't move. Instead, he looked at her father as if expecting something.

Her father gave Dev a glance that almost seemed… Guilty? "What did you want to discuss?" he asked.

Lacey looked around her at the familiar surroundings, at her mother's blond perfection, the refuge of her father's broad-shouldered frame.

The air vibrated with anger. With secrets.

"Someone explain to me what's happening here." She wrapped her hands around her middle.

Dev swore darkly and stepped toward her, his hands extended as if to hold her.

"Dev? What does he mean? Why would you want to—" *Use me?* She couldn't say it. "After last night, I thought we—"

Her father exploded. Whirled on Dev. "You were with her last night? Is there nothing you won't do for revenge?"

Dev's eyes shot sparks. He glanced at Lacey, then back at her father. Guilt rode hard on his face.

He turned toward her. "Lacey, don't let him lie

to you again. Remember what he did before. Last night has nothing to do with this.''

She wanted to run, wanted to hide from the foreboding sinking into her bones. Wanted to vanish right now, this instant. She held on desperately to the fraying edges of her strength. ''What doesn't have anything to do with last night?''

His green eyes darkened. His hands dropped to his sides. He turned to her father. ''Do you tell her, or do I?''

''Tell me what, Daddy?'' Her heart was thumping so fast she felt dizzy. ''Mother?''

Her mother looked utterly confused. Her father said nothing.

Dev crossed the floor then, came to her side. Grasped her arms and lowered her to the chair. His eyes looked so sad.

Whatever it was, she already knew she didn't want to hear it. Something deep and visceral told her she would never be the same once she did.

''No.'' She tried to rise, shaking her head. ''No, don't. I don't want to know, whatever it is.''

Dev looked so torn, so weary. ''This doesn't have to be bad, Lacey. There's good news for you.''

It didn't feel good. Her father looked a hundred years old.

Dev reached for her hands, clasped them tightly. His jaw tightened, and sorrow washed over his face. The green eyes she loved—

Dear God. She was such a fool. He didn't love her. He'd seen her heart tumble and he was—

''Don't,'' he said, his voice unbearably gentle. ''Don't try to imagine. In all of this, you're the innocent, Lacey.'' Then his voice thickened. ''But first, you have to believe me that last night was a miracle. It was a dream I'd given up on a long time ago. I want to believe that we laid a foundation that even this news can't destroy.''

She could barely concentrate on his words for the loud thumping of her heart. ''I don't understand.''

Dev cursed softly. ''I tried to figure out the right way to do this, but—''

''Just do it, Dev. Stop scaring me.''

''All right.'' He pinned her with that green gaze, his eyes soft and gentle but dark with foreboding. ''You're adopted, Lacey. I've been hired by your birth family to find you. You're not the natural child of the DeMilles.''

For a moment she didn't react at all. She blinked once, twice, then shook her head.

Then she surprised herself. She laughed, though she could hear the sharp edge of hysteria. ''What? You're out of your mind. What kind of joke is this?''

''It's not a joke.'' He shoved one hand through his hair. ''You are the natural child of Dalton Wheeler and Jenny Wallace Gallagher, both deceased. These people—'' he indicated her parents ''—paid a lot of money to hide your adoption and fake your birth records. You have a half sister, Maddie Rose Gallagher—Dalton's daughter—and two half brothers, Boone and Mitch Gallagher, who are Jenny's sons.''

Lacey jerked her hands away from his, rose again to pace. ''Stop. Stop now, Dev. This isn't funny.''

''I know it's not, sweetheart. I—'' He cursed

softly. His eyes locked on hers. "Listen to me— they're wonderful people, and they badly want to meet you. You're all the family Maddie has left."

"My parents wouldn't do that. My parents love me. You're telling me they've lied to me all my life. You're telling me I don't belong to them, that my whole life is a sham." She couldn't look at them yet. She had to make him stop saying these things. Dev was making a mockery of last night, and she still couldn't understand why he would want to do it.

"It's not a sham, sweetheart. You're still the same person. Don't you remember that you told me you never quite felt like you belonged?"

"Don't you dare use my own words against me."

"I'm not—" Dev wanted to touch her, to hold her. He'd botched this badly, and he needed to talk to her alone—but that wasn't going to happen.

"Think of what your father did to us." The very thought still made Dev's blood simmer. "Do you think a man like that would hesitate to lie to protect your mother's all-fired superiority? He's not going to tell the world that his blue-blooded princess isn't his but the child of two poor country kids from Morning Star." He stepped closer. "You should be glad you're not his blood."

She heard her mother's soft gasp, saw Margaret's delicate hand jerk upward before she dropped it to her lap, clenched bone-white. For a second, Lacey thought she saw moisture gather in her mother's eyes.

Impossible.

Desperately, Lacey turned to look at her father, to let him tell her it was indeed a joke. She was already preparing her rebuttal.

And then her gaze met her father's. She saw his face go ashen.

Her parents exchanged one look, only one.

But it was enough.

She fell back a step, her hand rising to her throat. "No," she whispered, feeling bile rise.

Dev stepped closer, reached for her.

"Get away from me, Dev." Was that her voice, so low and feral?

"Let me hold you, Lacey. Let me tell you about your family. They're wonderful people. Maddie was a well-known chef in Manhattan. I've eaten at her restaurant and it was the best food you ever put in your mouth."

She covered her ears, her voice turning shrill. "I don't want to hear about them. They have nothing to do with me."

"She has your eyes. She's your younger sister, and both of you have those same eyes, the same mouth. Don't you want to meet her?"

She'd backed against the wall, trying to escape the news. She sank to the floor, tears pouring down her cheeks.

Dev couldn't stand it, couldn't bear how her eyes looked so destroyed. He picked her up, but she came alive in his arms, striking out with nails, hitting his chest, her head whipping back and forth as strange little moans issued from her throat.

"Stop it." He shook her lightly, but she scratched his cheek with one nail. He bundled her into his arms, holding her so close that she couldn't do any more damage.

She went rigid against him.

Then she started trembling.

She jerked away, as though she feared him. Of all the things he'd imagined, he'd never imagined this. *Hate me, Lacey. Hit me, hurt me—but don't fear me.*

He let her go, something inside him dying.

Lacey turned toward the door, heart racing. She heard her father's voice, rough and cracking. "Good girl. Stay away from him. He's out for revenge. He's trying to blame his father's disgrace on me."

Lacey whirled. "What?"

"Leave her alone, DeMille. She doesn't need that to deal with, too."

Her father seemed to have recovered some of his strength. "Ask Devlin if he didn't come here today to threaten me. He's out to avenge his father. He used you, just like he was using you when you were kids. He hated me then, he hates me now. Ask him. Ask him if he didn't seduce you because you were my daughter. This is all about getting back at me."

Lacey shot a look at Dev. Saw the arrow hit its target.

"Lacey—" Dev's voice sounded wrecked. Desolate. "He's responsible for my father's death."

Not, "He's wrong." Not "He's lying."

He's responsible for my father's death. Ample motive for revenge. The best.

Lies swirled around her. Lies and vengeance and

horrible truths. She was a fraud. Her whole life was a lie.

Dev was a lie. Last night was a lie.

She was nothing. No one. And she was all alone. If she couldn't trust her parents, who could she trust?

She risked one look at Dev. His dark, ravaged face softened with something that looked far too much like—

Pity. He pitied her.

"Lacey—" She'd never heard her mother sound lost or helpless. "Lacey, don't leave—"

She turned back, looking at two people she realized she had never really known.

"But he's not lying about my birth, is he? Why, Daddy? Was I so unacceptable as I was? Were you ashamed? How could you? My whole life, all of it, is a lie. You—"

Before she broke down, she had to get out of here. Had to go somewhere she could think, could figure out what to do next. All she could think to do was move blindly toward the door.

Dev followed her. "Lacey, let me take you home. You're upset. I understand."

She slapped his hand away. Snarled. "Go to the devil, all of you. You don't understand. None of you do. My whole life I've never been able to look in a mirror and see that I looked like someone I knew. I never understood why—but now I do, don't I?"

Her heart cracking inside her chest, Lacey looked at them, thinking with a crazy kind of clarity that she finally understood why being a DeMille was such a struggle for her.

"I'm not really one of you," she said, marveling. A hollow little laugh escaped her throat. "No wonder I can't be perfect like you, Mother."

"Lacey, we're your parents. We're your family. Don't listen to him. We'll talk," her mother soothed. "You'll understand—"

Her father broke in. "You can't possibly take the word of this good-for-nothing—"

"Leave her alone," Dev roared. "Can't you see what you're doing to her? Stop making her choose."

"Stop it—all of you, stop it!" Lacey's stomach was on fire. "Leave me alone. Just—leave me alone." She flung open the door and raced through it. Ran to her car as though demons chased her.

Demons did.

As her tires screamed down around the curve and onto the street, Lacey wondered. *Who am I?*

But there was no one to give her the answer, except the couple who had betrayed her...and the man who had ruined her life for revenge.

And at the scene of her devastation, Dev cast one heated glance backward.

Margaret DeMille had abandoned her proud posture. Bent like an old woman, she sobbed softly. Dev could almost feel sorry for her—almost. Then he thought about the last look on Lacey's face.

He turned to the man who had wreaked such havoc. "I hope you're happy," he growled.

"You stay away from her. This is all your fault."

Dev's jaw clenched. "You go ahead and try to believe that. She's turned herself inside out to please you, and it was never enough. You've robbed both of us of years of happiness." Dev headed for the door, desperate to follow her.

At the door he turned back, pinning his oldest enemy with a glare that could melt lead. "If you ever hurt her again—ever lie to her again to save your own hide—I'll do everything in my power to make sure you never see her again. She's got a good family waiting for her. They'll accept her and love her, just as she is."

"She won't want to see you, either, Marlowe." DeMille wasn't giving up without a fight.

"Maybe not." Dev drew in a deep breath and tried not to think about the pain of losing her once more. "But she'll have to tell me that herself. I'm not abandoning her, ever again. I should have fought you harder last time, but I was just a kid and you held all the cards."

His fists clenched. "You have no power over me now, DeMille, and I'm not leaving. I'll protect her from a distance, if that's how it has to be—but I am never, ever walking away from her again."

Not until Lacey herself tells me she doesn't want me.

And even then, not without a fight. He'd missed too many years with the only woman he would ever love.

Chapter Eleven

Lacey didn't go home. There she would have to see the bed where Dev had made love to her with such power, with a tenderness that even now ripped all the way to her heart. She would have to see him in every corner, smell his scent on her pillow, remember his touch, his taste—

A car stopped suddenly in front of her, and she jerked herself to attention. Her whole body was shaking, and she needed to get off the road before she fell apart. But where to go?

She was so alone. So adrift.

She didn't know anything anymore. Who to trust, what to believe. Her life was quicksand, and no one was around to save her.

Lacey looked around and realized that she was near the foster home where Christina was living.

To hold that sweet child, to bury her face in Christina's bright hair, to cuddle her close and let the child's kindness soothe her—

No. She couldn't show up this distraught. Christina had too much to contend with already.

And Lacey understood, in a way she never had before, just how the little girl felt. Abandoned. Alone. Everything familiar lost.

She pulled to the curb, realizing that her dream of adopting Christina was only a fantasy now. She had no job to support her. She didn't feel right about keeping her trust fund, her town house, her car—they belonged to an impostor. All of it should go back to the people who'd been so ashamed of who she really was.

They'd loved her, she'd thought. But they'd lied to her with every breath. Everything she thought she knew about herself was a hoax. She was no princess, no River Oaks DeMille. She was a phony, a child who'd been given away. They'd considered her unworthy of the truth.

So where did that leave her? What was the truth of her life? If she wasn't Lacey DeMille in blood and bone, who was she?

Her stomach was on fire. She curled into a ball against the pain and willed herself to stop thinking. *Slow, deep breaths. Calm down. Have to calm down.*

She had no idea where she would go, where she belonged. She wanted to go back, to forget what had happened, to resume the life she'd once found wanting, but that life was forever beyond her reach.

How could she possibly face anyone in her old life now? She was a fake.

One step. One thing at a time. Drive back. Get some sleep. Don't try to figure it all out yet.

Boneless with exhaustion, Lacey put the car in gear and headed for the place that was no longer home.

Dev was going crazy. Houston was huge, sprawling for miles in every direction. He'd been by her house three times, driven everywhere he'd ever seen her go. He couldn't find her, didn't know where she was or what she was doing in her ravaged state.

A chill invaded his bones at the thought that she was out there somewhere alone. He'd seen her devastation, seen the way she'd held that fragile body together by sheer will as she escaped. He wanted to hold her, to shield her, to protect her from the pain.

It was one of life's nasty little ironies that he'd proven to be the chink in her armor. That he'd been the one to bring her down from princess to peasant, who'd been the bridge from heaven to hell. It seemed a century ago instead of only last night that she'd been naked beneath him, that he'd held her heart in his hands. That they'd been one.

Dev knew all about how a life could shatter. That he would be the instrument of her destruction was a cruel joke, but he wouldn't lie to himself about who was at fault. It had been his desire for revenge that had first brought Lacey into the line of fire between himself and her father.

He'd never expected to fall in love with the princess years ago.

Nor wanted to find out last night that love had not died.

And now here she was, the innocent sacrificed to pay for old debts, old anger, old betrayals.

The one most hurt—and the only one blameless.

Dev's jaw clenched as he turned to head back toward her town house once more. He had to find her. Had to replace the family he'd torn away with the family he knew would envelop her with love.

She wouldn't want to see him. DeMille was right. And it was only fair that his own heart pay the price.

Whatever he must pay, even if it be Lacey's eternal hatred, he could not rest until he'd given her back a life to replace the one he had destroyed.

It would be the worst kind of torture to be near her, knowing he could never have her, but he'd forfeited his right to her heart by his own actions, by setting the wheel in motion years ago to gain revenge without considering who might be hurt.

Revenge is a dish best served cold. He'd heard that somewhere. But no one had ever told him what it could cost the revenge seeker.

Charles DeMille must be laughing now. In the end, he'd taken everything Dev had ever wanted, including the only woman Dev would ever love.

She moved toward her bedroom, but stopped dead still in the doorway. Just looking at that bed and the shambles she and Dev had made of it hurt so badly she could barely breathe.

Memory after memory rolled over her in waves. The strength in his arms, the hot, sweet passion of his touch. The feel of him inside her after so many years' waiting.

She'd given herself to him so trustingly, welcomed him to her deepest self. How could he betray her like this? He'd known, all along, about the truth. Every second that he'd spent heating her skin with his kisses, driving the breath from her lungs with the power of his wanting.

He'd known. Known it would hurt her. During that magical date, he'd looked at her over and over, yet all she'd seen was longing.

Because that's what she'd wanted to see?

Backing away from her bedroom as though it were a den of snakes, Lacey all but crawled to the sofa and huddled against a chill that couldn't be explained by the sixty-odd degrees outside.

Who was she, if she wasn't a true DeMille?

It would explain everything, if it were true. Why she'd never felt like she truly fit. Why her mother pressed so hard for her to be perfect.

Because she was a mongrel of some sort.

Two poor country kids from Morning Star. Was that what he'd said?

Where was Morning Star?

And who did she come from? Why had she been so easy to give up?

Lacey thought she remembered Dev explaining, but her mind had been careening like a drunk. She'd missed most of what he said as the litany fired through her brain. *It's not true. It can't be true. I know who I am—why are you lying?*

She has your eyes.

A sister. She had a sister? For years and years, she'd prayed for one. Had imagined one at her tea parties. While playing dress-up. At night when she went to bed alone.

And had Dev mentioned brothers?

It hurt too much. She couldn't bear it.

But she wanted to know their names.

No. She didn't. Not if she had to ask Dev.

Why had he showered her with sweetness, set fire to her blood…shown her rapture? Why had Dev lied to her with every breath?

Revenge was a potent motive. One of the best.

Lacey's stomach burned, but she couldn't bear entering that bedroom again to get a new roll of antacids. Carefully, she forced her mind to empty, her breathing to slow.

Concentrate on the painting over the fireplace. Not on people. Not on what's happened.

With careful, steady discipline, Lacey aped the woman who wasn't really her mother…and summoned her formidable will to the aid of her rebellious stomach.

Finally, wrung out and exhausted, she dozed.

When she awoke, she was logy, muzzy with sleep. The fire in her belly had died to embers, and in its place was a longing that mocked her. She realized that, despite everything, the only person she wanted to see, the only one she thought would understand, was Dev. He hadn't liked her money, had encouraged her at every step to break away from the life that had stifled her.

But all along, she'd been only a means to an end.

A way to get back at her father for another grievous wrong.

She didn't doubt now that her father—that Charles had done something terrible to Dev's father. Whatever it was, she was sorry for all he and his family had suffered.

But she was even more sorry that Devlin Marlowe had ever stepped back into her life—and wrecked it.

You said you didn't fit. You said you wanted something more. Here's your chance, she told herself.

Lacey tried to summon the energy to feel liberated, to rejoice that she was free to choose. She should thank them all, she realized. They'd freed her. Old loyalties, old responsibilities…old dreams—all were useless. All were the past, fractured from the present like a fault line divides the land.

But all she felt was tired to the bone.

Her future lay ahead, an empty road.

But it was shrouded in mist, and Lacey had no map.

She was there at last, thank God, but she wasn't answering her phone.

Dev was going to knock. If she didn't answer the door, he was going to pick her locks. It might be illegal, but he didn't care. He had to know that she was all right.

That she wasn't planning something drastic.

Dev damned his palms for sweating. She'd better be angry. She'd better be spitting fire.

He didn't think he could bear to see her so fragile again. So much like a baby's breath could knock her down.

She might not want to see him, but he had to know that she wasn't in trouble. He didn't mind looking like ten kinds of fool if only he could find her inside painting her toenails.

He'd bet the farm that she wasn't.

Lacey heard the pounding but ignored it. She had learned to ignore the ringing of the phone. She'd had to seek the antacids, after all, then she'd donned her oldest, most comforting nightgown. All she wanted now was to sleep, but sleep seemed a million miles away.

The pounding stopped, mercifully. Lacey rolled over and tried to find a comfortable spot on a bed that still smelled of Dev and long, slow loving. The scent of him, the memories... They broke her heart.

Then she heard the door open, and that same heart began to race.

Footsteps echoed down the polished wooden hallway floor. Her bedroom door burst open, and there he stood.

"A new look for you, princess." Dev forced calm into his voice and leaned against the doorjamb lazily, trying to still his rapid pulse. When she hadn't answered, he'd been unable to erase the thought that he might find her lifeless, that he'd be responsible for sending her over the edge.

"Go away," she said too quietly.

She looked like hell, but she was breathing. Blessed anger did a tap dance through his veins. He strolled to her bedside and studied her, shocked at the damage. Her skin was translucent, her eyes dark holes in her face.

The fault lay squarely at his doorstep. He had started her down the road to this hell.

He had to find a way to bring her back.

His apologies would have to wait. She was too raw to talk about this now, even if he had any idea what to say. She needed the basics first.

"When's the last time you ate?"

"I don't know." Her voice was hollow. He'd sell his soul to hear that snotty princess-to-peasant tone right now.

Without a moment's hesitation, he swept her up in his arms and strode across the room.

She stirred only faintly. "How did you get in here?"

"I picked your locks," he drawled. "Wanna make something of it?" He kept striding, heading back toward her kitchen. Once there, he set her down on the counter between refrigerator and sink. "Answer me—when's the last time you ate something?"

"I don't know...the picnic at the museum maybe," she whispered. Her eyes were dull and haunted.

Dev wanted to smash something. Wanted to howl out his own anguish.

"Go away, Dev." Her voice broke.

His heart cracked right along with it. Ruthlessly, he clamped down on the urge to fall to his knees. "The phone's over there. Call nine-one-one. I'm not leaving." He bent down and began rummaging through her refrigerator.

"What are you doing?"

He straightened, holding eggs, milk, butter and cheese in his hands. With two long strides, he crossed to the island and dumped his booty.

She started to get down.

"You move from that spot and you'll regret it." His voice went fierce.

She didn't respond. She was scaring the hell out of him.

"I broke into your house. Don't you care?"

She didn't answer, staring at the floor.

Dev studied the part in her hair and wished she would scream at him, curse him—anything but this defeat.

He decided to push. "I know you're a pampered princess, but surely you have more guts than this."

Her head rose swiftly, the quick spark of anger the best thing he'd seen in days. "Get out of my house."

Then he grinned, quick and crooked and rakish. "Make me."

When she slid off the counter, her knees buckled. In a split second, he was by her side, steadying her against him.

"Sit down. Damn it, sit down." Fear made him rough. He helped her to a chair, then carefully stepped back because he wanted to hold her too much. "I'll have an omelette ready in a minute."

Lacey watched him, those big eyes studying his every move. "I don't know what to do," she said so softly he almost didn't hear it.

Dev wondered then just how many times a heart could break. How he could ever fix this.

When he could finally speak, his voice was gentle. "Eat first, Lacey. Let your mind rest."

He scooped the omelette onto a plate and poured her a glass of milk, setting both in front of her. Pulling out the chair beside her and turning it backward, he straddled it. When she made no move, he picked up the fork.

She opened her mouth to speak, but he was too quick with a forkful of omelette.

"No more talking. Eat."

Rebellion leaped into her eyes.

He welcomed the heat, the spark. She would need all of it and more as she rebuilt her life.

Then Lacey opened her mouth. The sight of those lips parted...the pink of her tongue—

Memory scorched Dev down to his toes.

When she took the fork from his hands and averted her gaze from his, Dev was painfully aware of what he'd lost.

But at least Lacey was eating her eggs.

"You need to sleep. I'll clean up." Dev took her clean plate and headed for the sink.

The relief from that piercing green gaze was welcome. Every bite had come at a cost, but Lacey knew he was right. The basics were important. She had decisions to make, a new life to build.

The burning returned.

She wanted to sink into the comforting darkness of sleep, to see if all this would vanish before she must wake.

But that's what she'd always done. Hide behind what was proper, what was safe.

She couldn't sleep yet. "I want answers, Dev."

He finished loading the dishwasher and took his time drying his hands before he turned. For a long moment he watched her, his expression shifting from the dark shadows of guilt to a painful longing—and back again.

Why, Dev? Why was revenge more important than my love?

His gaze dropped to the hand that was rubbing her stomach. "Why don't you sleep first?" he asked gently.

Suddenly she was furious at him, at all of them for thinking they knew what was best for her. "You didn't care enough to be honest with me—don't you tell me what I need," she snapped.

He looked as though she'd slapped him. Strong fingers raked through his black hair, shoving that rebellious lock backward.

It sprang forward again, spilling over his forehead. Then his face closed up. "I don't expect you to understand what—"

She leaped to her feet. "Oh, no—God forbid anyone should think that the poor little rich girl has any backbone. She's such a hothouse flower that she can't possibly take care of herself or know her own mind." The torpor that had sunk its claws into her vanished like mist in the sun. Other claws dug in now—talons of anger, of resentment, of the bitter knowledge that she'd drifted through her life and let everyone else call the shots.

She paced the kitchen, one hand tightly gripping the fabric over her middle. Humiliation burned all the way up to her throat. "You made a mockery of me, Devlin Marlowe. I want you to tell me what my father—what Charles DeMille did to your father that was important enough to take my heart and rip it open.''

''Lacey, calm down. Your stomach is hurting, isn't it? You need—''

''Don't you tell me what I need. You don't know what I need. I thought you would understand, but you couldn't possibly understand me and do that to me—'' Razor-sharp pain ripped through her, and she bent over.

Dev moved toward her.

Lacey held her palm out in warning. ''You stay away.'' Her voice turned almost feral, half wild with pain. ''You stand over there and you explain to me what he did. You admit to me that I was only a means to an end.''

Dev's hands lifted from his sides. She couldn't bear the look in his green eyes.

''Admit it, damn you!'' She forced herself to straighten against the pain. Her voice dropped lower. ''And then you explain to me why you made love to me like that. How you could lie to me with every caress.'' Half blind with tears, she backed away from him, then felt the wall at her back.

Dev looked suddenly older. The devilish rake was gone. In its place was a man full of shadows.

He exhaled in a gust, his shoulders sinking.

The look on his face made her wrap her arms tightly around her middle.

''I did set out to seduce you back then, Lacey. I wanted to ruin the one thing Charles DeMille held most special, his pampered princess. He'd made it clear that we were beneath him and his blue-blooded family. I wanted to make him pay for every bit of charity he'd forced down our throats, for every time he'd made me feel worthless.''

His eyes hurt her to look at them. Her stomach was on fire. She started to walk away, unable to hear any more, but he grabbed her arm and whirled her back.

''That's how it started, Lacey—but that's not how it ended. My brilliant strategy blew up in my face when you turned out to be something so special and rare that even a revenge-seeking, hormone-driven boy could recognize it.'' He dropped his hand. ''I'm not proud of what I intended, but you need to know that I was so sick with love for you that it nearly killed me when you threw my love on the ground that night and walked away.''

Harsh laughter scraped from his throat. ''It was my just deserts, I guess. But I wanted you, God, how I wanted you. You were the finest, most precious thing I'd ever known. You have to believe that, if you believe nothing else.''

She was so tired, so ravaged by emotion. Lacey wanted to burrow somewhere into the darkness until the nerve endings weren't so raw. Wanted to flee the live coals burning from the inside out.

She looked at this man before her and saw the teenager who had stolen her heart, then left without a word. The man who'd given her the most romantic night of her life, made love to her like something out of a dream—

Then dropped the bombshell that had exploded her life.

"How can I? After this, how?" She stared at him. "I loved you, Dev," she whispered. "I would have done anything for you—"

Dev laughed, and the sound of it was like grating metal. "You didn't give all this up seventeen years ago—" He swept an arm out to include her luxurious surroundings. "You didn't defy them for me then." On his face was the bitterness that must have been festering all this time.

The burning inside her belly spread to her heart. Her vision grayed.

"Don't lie to me, Lacey." His voice was low and fierce. "Don't lie to yourself. I begged you to come with me. You chose them."

Her father had been right. Dev had every reason to want revenge.

Suddenly, jagged claws tore her open. The pain was so blinding that Lacey couldn't hear any more, couldn't see any more. Everything vanished behind a red haze of agony.

She bent over double and sank to the floor with a cry.

Chapter Twelve

Dev closed the distance in one long stride, pulling Lacey close. Her arms clutched her stomach; her whole body locked in a spasm. "Is it your stomach? Talk to me, damn it. Who's your doctor?"

"I—I'll be fine," she answered, her face ash-white, her jaw locked against the pain.

"Tell me your doctor's name. This has gone on long enough. Don't you know how dangerous it is to play around with an ulcer?"

"It's not an ulcer. It'll go away," she whispered through clenched teeth. But she curled into him, and a tiny moan escaped.

"Fine. Don't tell me. You're going to let someone look at you." Dev picked her up and headed for the door.

Two minutes later, Lacey was lying in the back

seat of his car, curled up in a ball. He'd gotten her doctor's name from her parents' butler Murphy and they were racing toward Methodist Hospital. Her doctor would meet them there. Murphy had promised not to tell the DeMilles yet—not until Lacey could decide if she wanted to see them. The last thing she needed was something else to upset her. In return, Dev had promised to call the old man the minute he knew anything.

"Hold on, sweetheart," Dev said, reaching back between the seats to clasp her hand.

Lacey gripped his hand with a strength he didn't know she had.

I'm sorry, he wanted to say. *Sorry I upset you, sorry I involved you, sorry I—*

The list was too long and time might be too short. *Please,* he begged whatever forces might be listening. *Give me the chance to make it up to her. Let her be okay.*

Then they were at the hospital. Dev pulled in close to the emergency entrance, out of the way of emergency vehicles but not caring what happened to his car. All that mattered was Lacey, getting her help now.

Gathering her up in his arms, he ran for the door, steeling himself not to let his fear for her keep him from thinking straight.

But she was so fragile. So wounded.

They had to pry her out of his arms, but Dev drew the line at waiting outside when Lacey gripped his hand, looking frightened. "I'll stay out of the way, but I'm not leaving. Go ahead and call security—just get ready for the guard to be your next patient.''

"Are you family?" the nurse asked.

Impotent fury kept him barely civil. "I'm all she's got right now."

"Sir, you've got to move away. Please—we need you to give us some answers. And the patient needs privacy."

Her face stark with pain, Lacey gripped his fingers while she turned to the emergency room physician. "Please let him stay."

Dev's heart thumped once, hard. "I've got to stand back so they can take care of you, sweetheart, but I'll be right over there." He gestured with his head. "All you have to do is call out. I am not leaving you, do you hear me?"

Her eyes were huge and glassy with fear, but she nodded.

"Everything's going to be fine." Dev kissed her knuckles, then let her hand go. It was the hardest thing he'd ever done to step away.

It wasn't easy finding a spot to be out of the way but still be within her sight, but Dev managed the dance. Every time Lacey's eyes darted toward him, it was all he could do not to shove everyone out of his path. His reaction was primitive, he knew. He kept a rein on it, just barely.

"Sir, please—I need some information," a clerk requested.

"Shoot." Dev never gave her a glance, his eyes focused only on Lacey.

He'd pushed her to this point, and he'd have to live with knowing that. She might never forgive him, but right now, his only concern was getting her through this.

If only she didn't look so frail, gripped so hard by agony. He should have forced her to do something about it sooner. Shouldn't have let her pass it off as nothing.

Shouldn't have gotten her involved in this nightmare in the first place—how about that, Devlin? She's the innocent, and she's the one writhing in pain. She's the one whose world you blew apart.

Dev rubbed his eyes, gritty with exhaustion, and asked the clerk to repeat the question.

A few hours later, Dev strode toward her room. They'd given her something that made her drowsy, then admitted her for observation. She'd fallen asleep holding his hand, and he'd slipped out to make some calls. Tomorrow they'd run more tests, but her doctor had already confirmed what Dev had suspected.

Close. Too close. The years of pressure to live up to the DeMilles' impossible standards and her own had taken their toll. Lacey had an ulcer—the only question was how bad. If she let it go too far, it could kill her.

Her doctor had told Dev that he'd tried to warn her, tried to find a way to get her help. She'd refused any sort of medication, denying that she'd been a bundle of nerves for years.

Then her doctor had told him that Lacey was to be kept calm at all costs. He'd agreed, after Dev had explained in confidence about the shocks Lacey had sustained, to call the DeMilles and ask them to stay away until Lacey asked for them.

He'd also made it very clear that Dev himself was on probation, warning that he'd have Dev barred from her room if he upset her.

Dev had called Murphy first, to ease the old man's mind. Then he'd called Maddie and explained the whole sorry situation. It was a credit to Maddie's compassion that she hadn't told him to go to hell, especially since he still couldn't promise her that Lacey would want to see any of them.

Maddie had said they'd be in Houston by nightfall. She'd agreed not to push it, to bide their time. She seemed to recognize that the trip could be for nothing, but she and Boone insisted on being there, just in case. Mitch and his fiancée, Perrie, were in Dallas buying clothes for their wedding and honeymoon, but she would leave word for them to follow.

Now as he strode toward Lacey's room, however, Dev's only thought was for her. What he would say, how he could ever make it up to her for all the anguish.

He slipped inside quietly and crossed to the bed. They'd warned him that she would be dopey—but she would be relaxed. Very relaxed. He never wanted to see her in that kind of agony again.

Dev studied her as she lay there so still. Her hair was tousled like someone had run an eggbeater through it, mascara was smudged beneath her lashes, and her lips were unpainted.

He'd never seen a more beautiful sight in his life. He wanted to touch her so much, but she needed rest. With trembling fingers, he brushed faintly over her hair.

All of a sudden, everything blurred. Dev squeezed the bridge of his nose and fought the memories.

He'd hurt her so badly. Even if she forgave him, he wasn't sure he'd ever forgive himself. To the end of his days, he'd be haunted by the look of betrayal on her face.

Dev moved away from the bed, away from temptation. He'd keep watch—he'd guard her with his life, if needed. But he'd forfeited all rights to anything more when he'd lied to himself as well as to her.

She was more than a job. More than a duty to friends. More than a challenge—more important than any revenge.

Too late for it to matter, Dev realized that Lacey was simply...everything.

Lacey tried to escape from the dream but the darkness enveloped her...surrounded her with mournful sobs and lonely sighs. She was lost, forever. Alone. Afraid. She searched in vain, reaching out with fingers that could touch nothing. Eyes that could not see.

At the edge of the forest she saw the glimmer of strawberry blond hair. Christina's eyes begged her, but the crone's claws stole her away, lost forever among the menacing dark trees.

You can't have her...you're no one...you don't exist. Phantom voices chanted. Shrill laughter split the air.

Off in the distance, she saw a man on a black charger, racing her way. Lacey tried to run to him, knowing he would help her, but the gnarled limbs of the trees trapped her.

Revenge, sighed the wind, curling around her ankles, sliding up her spine, chilling her to the bone.

The man and the horse neared, and Lacey cried out—

A hand clapped over her mouth, rendering her mute. Revenge...he only wants revenge...he doesn't want you....

Lacey clawed her way through the branches, certain that only he could help her, only he could save Christina. Only he could tell her the path—

The man raced closer, his green eyes dark and haunted.

Help me, Dev—

The hand muffled her screams.

And then Dev vanished.

Dev jerked awake in the chair, trying to figure out where he was.

Hospital. Lacey.

Then she moaned again. "Dev—"

He was on his feet in an instant.

Her head tossed from side to side. "Christina— help me. Don't leave. Dev, don't—"

"Shh," he murmured, taking her hand in his. "It's all right, Lacey. It's just a dream. You're okay."

Her lashes fluttered, then closed. Slowly, like a curtain, they rose. "Dev?" She gripped his hand like it was her last hope.

He smiled. "It's all right. You're in Methodist

Hospital. They're going to take good care of you.''
With one hand, he brushed the hair on her forehead.
"How do you feel?"

Lacey frowned. "Hospital? Why—" She shook
her head as if to unscramble her senses.

"They gave you something to make you sleep.
That's why you feel groggy." He gripped her hand
and resisted the urge to scoop her up and hold her
tightly. "Lacey, you came so close. Too close." He
heard the roughness in his voice. "They're going
to run tests tomorrow, but you can't keep ignoring
this. You've got an ulcer, and you're in danger."
He brushed her cheek. "You scared the hell out of
me."

He saw when she remembered. All of it. Her grip
slackened.

He stepped back, let her hand go. Closed his
mind to foolish dreams.

Lacey struggled to catch up. "Where are my—
where are Charles and Margaret? Do they know?"

He nodded. "Your doctor asked them to stay
away until you could decide whether or not to see
them." He turned away. "I'd better go tell the
nurse you're awake."

Lacey watched Dev's face close up, heard the
politeness in his tone. So remote. Almost a stranger
now.

She wanted to grasp his hand again and hold on
tight. He seemed the only thing familiar in her
world.

Then she remembered what he'd said before
she'd collapsed. Remembered the bitter disappointment on his face. *Don't lie to me...don't lie to*

*yourself. I begged you to come with me. You chose
them.*

She hadn't had the courage to reach out for what
she wanted then. Now she didn't know what she
wanted.

Except some answers.

"Why, Dev?" she asked quietly. Why did you
do it? Why did you lie?

He halted at the doorway, turning back slowly.
"Why what?" But she could see in his eyes that
he knew what she was asking.

He shook his head. "It doesn't matter now."
Resignation darkened his tone. "All that can matter
now is that you get well." He pulled open the door
and left.

There was nothing he could do for her that would
ever make up for the havoc he'd wreaked in her
life, but Lacey's nightmare ramblings had shown
him one way to make amends.

Christina. The little girl Lacey wanted to adopt.
Dev might not be able to put Lacey's old life back
to rights, but he could give her the ammunition to
make a new one, if she still wanted it.

It was hard to leave her behind, but the doctor
had already made it clear that the tests they would
run on her would take most of the day and he was
not welcome.

It would be Dev's self-imposed penance to be at
hand as much as possible until she was released.
Right there to watch how she suffered and be able
to do little or nothing to change it.

But Dev needed to do something constructive.

He stopped by Connor's apartment to shower and change, then got on the phone and started working.

Three hours later, he alighted from his car in front of a modest home. Christina's social worker, Louise Wardlow, was waiting on the porch.

"Mr. Marlowe, I don't have to tell you that you're an angel in my book. What you've accomplished in one morning would have taken us weeks—if we could ever get the time at all." Her wise brown eyes gauged him carefully, despite her words. "You mind telling me why you're doing this?"

Dev shrugged. "Let's just say that I owe Lacey and leave it at that."

The brown eyes didn't leave his. "Why do I think there's a lot more to the story? You got the look of a man with some worries."

"If I do, they're no one's fault but my own." He nodded toward the door. "Thank you for letting me meet Christina."

"I like the look of you, Devlin Marlowe. I think you're a man who can see past the surface. Christina's heart is a good one. Her face doesn't change that."

"Lacey cares about her. That's all I need to know."

She put one hand on his arm as he headed toward the door. "Is Lacey going to be all right?" All she knew was that Lacey was in the hospital.

"I hope so," he said grimly. "She's got to ease up on herself."

"Ain't that the truth? That girl's too sensitive for

work like this—but she's good with the children. Just eats her up inside.''

''Mrs. Wardlow—''

''Louise, hon. We're already way past that.''

Dev grinned for the first time in hours. ''Louise, if Christina wants to go, do you think she could visit Lacey? Lacey's worried about her.''

The woman patted his shoulder. ''We can do that. God knows where I'll fit it into my schedule, but I *will* make time for that. Christina needs to see her, too.''

Dev nodded. ''Thank you.'' He pulled open the screen door and held it for her.

Once inside, Dev glanced around the worn but spotless house. Toys were scattered everywhere and the furniture was shabby, but the place smelled clean and every surface was covered with pictures of children.

Foster parents were surely one of the world's kindest blessings. To take a child not one's own and care for that child fully, knowing you might have to give the child up in a matter of days or months, required a special kind of human being.

''Hello.'' The woman who greeted them was small and rounded, her hair caught carelessly back in a plain rubber band. Dev saw kindness in her eyes. ''I'm Helen Carpenter.''

The social worker spoke first. ''Helen, this is Devlin Marlowe. He's helping us on Christina's case.''

''Thank you for seeing me, Mrs. Carpenter.''

Her smile was warm but her gaze worried. ''You're here to meet Christina?''

Dev knew he could only put them at ease by his actions, not his words. "Yes, ma'am. Please."

Around the doorway, a strawberry-blond head appeared. Huge dark eyes followed. Slowly and shyly, the little girl made her way into the room.

Dev lowered himself to his heels and smiled. "Hello, Christina. Lacey's told me a lot about you."

She studied him carefully. Dev didn't try to avoid her uneven features. He looked at her straight on.

There is nothing so discerning as a child's impulse toward honesty. "Did she tell you my face is crooked?"

His heart filled. "Yes." He continued in a neutral tone. "My face is crooked, too. See my nose?" He pointed toward the bump.

"Did somebody hit you, too?" she whispered.

At that moment, Dev would have liked to tear the guy limb from limb. How anyone could harm a child—

"Yep." He nodded. "You know what else Lacey told me?"

Christina took another step toward him. "What?"

"She told me about your beautiful heart. Crooked faces can be fixed, you know, but ugly hearts never mend. Looks to me like you've got what's important."

The little girl cocked her head and studied him. Finally, she spoke up. "Is Lacey going to be all right?"

I hope so. God, I hope so. But Dev didn't voice his worries. "She'd feel better if she could see you.

Mrs. Wardlow says she would take you, if it's all right with Mrs. Carpenter.''

Christina leaned over and whispered, ''Hospitals are scary.''

Dev hadn't thought about that, about her past experiences. ''Lacey would understand if you didn't want to come.''

The big brown eyes looked conflicted. ''Would you be there?''

''Would you want me to?''

Blond curls bounced. ''Please.''

Dev held out his hand. ''It's a deal.''

Lacey lay back in the bed, drained from the day's exhausting round of tests. Her doctor's warnings still rang in her ears.

I don't care if you have to walk away from every person you know, young lady. You have to get squared away inside yourself. Diet, rest and medication will help, but they're just bandages on the wound. What you really need is to change your life so you're not so wound up all the time, trying to please everyone but Lacey.

You won't be so lucky next time. You've never seen a patient die before your eyes from a bleeding ulcer, but I'm telling you, that's where you're headed. Whatever is going on in your life, you make peace with it. Do you hear me?

Not so easy. But he was right—it was time for some choices.

Someone knocked on the door.

''Come in,'' she answered.

Dev poked his head around. "Is this a bad time?"

She wanted to banish this Dev forever, the one who was so polite, who had lost all devilment in his eyes. "No. I think they're through poking and prodding."

He walked inside, casting a quick glance behind him before the door shut. "What did the doctor say?"

"You want the whole lecture or just the highlights?"

His quick grin touched something deep inside her. If only his eyes matched it. "I might need some pointers for my own lecture."

She tried to smile at him, wanting so badly for him to come closer, to be the reckless Dev who'd dare anything. "Go ahead. I'm beaten into submission already."

He scanned her face. "You look tired. I can come back." He made as if to turn.

"No—please. Stay."

Dev settled into an uneasy stance. The silence between them was awkward as never before.

"Dev, I—"

"I have a surprise—" Both spoke at once.

"Go ahead." He gestured.

"No, that's okay—a surprise?" Then she pulled herself back just a fraction. "What is it?"

"I think you'll like it."

"All right."

Dev moved toward the door and pulled it open. A beloved blond head peered from behind him.

"Oh, Christina—" Joy leaped inside her.

Christina reached for Dev's hand and glanced at him for reassurance. He nodded and walked her to the bed. Louise Wardlow stepped into the room, nodding at Lacey and smiling widely.

Lacey returned the nod, but quickly shifted her gaze to the little girl.

"Dev said you wouldn't be so sad if I would come see you," Christina offered.

Dev, was it? How had this happened? She shot a quick glance at him, but his face was impassive. Lacey leaned down and tried to lift the girl. Dev picked her up and settled her on the bed beside Lacey.

Barely able to see past her tears, Lacey nodded. "I'm so happy to see you. I feel better already."

"Want a hug?"

"More than anything, sweetie." Lacey gathered the little girl into her arms, squeezing her eyes shut in thanksgiving. She opened them and tried to express to Dev silently what this meant. For one second, joy flared in those green eyes she treasured, then his face settled into remoteness again.

Lacey tried to push away her desolation and concentrate on the child. They began to talk.

Too few minutes later, she felt her strength waning. Christina chattered on, happily oblivious.

"Hey, muppet," Dev said. "I think it's time for Lacey's nap."

Louise spoke. "I'd like a minute with Lacey first, please."

She and Dev exchanged glances. He held out a hand to Christina. "How about you and I go see if we can scare up some ice cream?"

"Yippee!" Christina started to scoot off the bed, then stopped. "Sleep tight, Lacey."

Lacey gathered her in. "I will, sweetie. Thanks so much for coming to see me. I know hospitals aren't your favorite place."

"But Dev told me that it would make you feel better and that he'd be with me the whole time." Hero worship shone in her gaze.

So Dev was here for Christina's sake. Lacey couldn't be jealous of a child so in need of care. "He was right." She kissed Christina's cheek and helped her down. "See you soon, okay?"

Christina skipped over and grasped Dev's hand. "Okeydoke!" She turned her face up to him, eyes glowing. "Ready for ice cream?"

Dev grinned. "Always." With a quick nod toward Lacey, he ushered the child outside.

Louise shook her head fondly. "He's good with her. Really good."

"He half raised his own siblings, I think."

"Still, he handled her just right. Didn't look away from her, didn't give her pity. Just treated her normal, which is all the child wants." The older woman gazed steadily at Lacey. "A woman could have a good life with a man like that."

Lacey flushed. "I don't think that's in the cards, Louise."

"Not good enough for you, society girl?"

Lacey's temper flared. "I don't see that it's any of your business." Immediately, she was ashamed. What did Dev call it? Princess to peasant? "I'm sorry. Things are—complicated."

"Man-woman stuff generally is, hon. None of it

comes easy. But a man like that, a smart woman figures out how to keep him. Especially after all he did.''

''What do you mean?''

Louise settled a large brown envelope in her lap. ''All the proof you could want that Christina's aunt isn't good parent material. Seems the woman's got some brushes with the law, some real bad habits and some very unsavory friends. Nice courtin' gift, I'd say.''

Lacey clasped the envelope in her hands and ducked her head, blinking back tears. ''We're not courting,'' she whispered.

''Hmmph—fat lot you know. You're not watching that man's face when he's looking at you and thinks nobody's paying attention. He's got it bad, girl. Whatever it is that's gone wrong between you, there's plenty of feelings there to tide you over.''

Lacey lifted her head and studied the woman who'd seen so much of life's woes. Louise's own life had been worse than most of her cases.

How spoiled I am. How pampered. She's right. I'm soft. Dev deserved a chance to explain, at least.

Her fingers brushed the envelope. This was something the man who'd made love to her so tenderly would do.

It nearly killed me when you threw my love on the ground and walked away.

There had to be reasons he'd kept so much secret. She needed to hear him out.

''So you're telling me to fight for him?'' A tiny smile curved Lacey's lips.

''Don't know how you can look at yourself in

the mirror if you don't try. That's a lot of man there, girl. Big heart, fine and strong. Easy on the eyes, too.'' Louise grinned, eyes sparkling. ''You too soft for the fight, maybe I'll jump in and grab him for myself.''

Lacey laughed, and it felt so good. She settled back on the pillows. ''I think I've been feeling sorry for myself.''

Louise shrugged. ''Little bit of that goes a long way.''

Lacey drew a deep breath. ''You're right. It does.'' She looked carefully at the woman before her. ''I'm going to try to adopt Christina, if I can get the rest of my life straightened out. You might not want me working on her case until then.''

''I get worried about your behavior, I'll tell you. Meanwhile, you need to get yourself well. There's work to be done, and I'm not getting any younger.'' She made as if to leave.

Lacey held out the envelope. ''Here—you'll want this.''

Louise winked. ''Not my courtin' gift, hon. I best be leaving it with you. Seems like someone in this room might want to thank the man properly.'' She waved on her way out.

If only he'll come back so I can, Lacey thought. *If only I can dig past the remote stranger to find the real Dev.*

Chapter Thirteen

When the tap on the door turned out to be Dev, Lacey's nerves jittered. "Hi. Come on in." She clutched the envelope to her breast. "Thank you for getting her here."

He shrugged. "Happy to do it."

Still so distant. So impassive.

"And thank you for this—" She indicated the envelope. "Louise says that Christina's aunt can't make her case now. If only—"

He frowned faintly. "If only what?"

She glanced away. "I don't know if I'm the best person for Christina now. I don't know how I'll support her. None of what I thought was mine feels right to keep now."

"They're still your parents, Lacey. They

wouldn't want you to give up anything of yours. They still love you.''

''Do they, Dev? Why would you lie like that to someone you love?''

A spasm of pain crossed his face, and she regretted her words.

Before she could speak, he did. ''Your birth family is nothing to be ashamed of. Those people are as deep-down good as anyone I've ever known.'' Finally, the impassiveness gave way to strong feeling. ''You need to meet them and find out for yourself.''

Just the thought made her uneasy. She could listen, though. Find out more. ''Tell me about them.''

Dev thought for a minute, then a faint smile curved his lips. ''You'd love Maddie. She's funny and cheerful and about half Gypsy. And she'd understand, Lacey. She only found out a few months ago that her father lived under a fake name for her whole life.''

''What?''

''Thought you were unique, didn't you?'' A trace of a frown ghosted across his face. ''Maddie thought she was the only one left. She'd never known grandparents, and both her parents were dead. I found her for Boone's dad.''

''I don't understand.''

Some of the strain on his face eased as he slid into the story. ''Maddie's father—your father— Dalton Wheeler, took the rap for a murder he didn't commit. His stepfather, son of the most powerful man in the county, beat Dalton's mother brutally, and she killed him in self-defense. Dalton confessed in order to save her from jail, then vanished with the help of one of her friends so that she couldn't recant and sacrifice herself. He gave up his identity and the woman he loved—your mother, Jenny—to save his mother. Jenny, like everyone else in Morning Star, thought he was dead.''

Lacey couldn't take it all in. ''They were married?''

''No,'' Dev said. ''But they'd been in love since she was fourteen. Dalton disappeared without ever knowing she was pregnant.'' He looked at her intensely. ''Maddie is absolutely certain of that. He never really loved another woman, not even Maddie's mother, like he loved Jenny. After she went away to have you, Jenny came back and married Sam Gallagher, but she was never the same after she had to give you up. Boone and Mitch and Sam all remarked on the fact that there was always this sadness she couldn't shake. Until Maddie found her grandmother's diary with its speculations about the months that Jenny was gone from Morning Star, no one knew why.''

''They never knew about me?''

He shook his head and took her hand. ''She never told a soul. Both Boone and Mitch say she always talked about how much she wished for a daughter. But until I started looking, it was only a guess on your grandmother's part that you even existed.''

Grandmother. The only one Lacey had known had been Margaret's mother, stiff in her disapproval. ''What was her name?''

''Your grandmother?'' At her nod, he continued.

"Rose. Rose Wheeler. Maddie's middle name is Rose. You all have the same eyes. Dalton's eyes, too."

"What did—" Her voice failed her. "What did my mother look like?"

"She had blond hair and blue eyes like Boone's, but she was delicate like you. Maddie's taller, like her dad, but you and she share his coloring."

"Tell me about Mitch and Boone."

"They're both big men, a couple of inches taller than me. Boone used to be a Navy SEAL, but he's got a real reputation as a fine horseman. He loves that ranch. Says it's the only place he ever wanted to be. He and Maddie met when his dad willed her the ranch house—it was Dalton's old home place.

"Boone was madder than the devil, and the terms of the will said that he and Maddie had to live there for thirty days before he could buy her out." He grinned. "Maddie led him on a merry chase, but I think he was a goner the day he met her. They're married now.

"Mitch is a hunting and fishing guide. His hair is dark, and his eyes are brown like Sam's." He stared at her for a minute. "He's had a rough time of it. Jenny died in his arms after an accident, and he blamed himself for it. His father did, too— banned him from the funeral and banished him from their lives. Sam went about half crazy when Jenny died. Mitch has been alone for a long time, hadn't seen Boone since that day. I just found him right before I found you. But he's got a woman he's going to marry soon. Her name is Perrie, and she's got a five-year-old son named Davey who thinks Mitch hung the moon.''

Dev studied her. ''He's a good man, Lacey. They're all good people. They're waiting to welcome you into the family. Boone and Mitch swear that Jenny was just this side of an angel, and that she would never have given up a child unless she'd had no other choice. They want to do this for her, to bring her missing baby home. And Maddie— well, you're the only family Maddie has left.''

She couldn't fasten on the emotions of people she'd never met. Not yet. They weren't real. She wasn't sure she wanted them to be. ''I'm sorry.'' And she meant it. ''I just…it's a little hard to take in.''

He nodded, and that lock of black hair fell over his forehead again. She could remember how it felt against her skin.

''Were you surprised? When you found out that the baby was me, I mean?''

His head jerked up, his gaze meeting hers. For a precious moment, brilliant green glowed with wry humor. ''You can't imagine how much. Out of all the world…it had to be you.''

She smiled, but her own was tinged with rue, too. Then suddenly, her eyes filled. ''I don't know who I am, Dev. Maybe I should be glad that they're not my parents after what they did to you, but I'm not.'' She lifted her head. ''I'm nothing now. No one. Don't you see? I don't belong anywhere.''

He touched her hand, then pulled away as though her skin burned him. But his eyes focused intently on hers. ''You need to do this. You need to see the place where your roots are buried. Need to meet the people who share your blood.''

''I—'' She glanced away. ''I don't know—''

''They're here.''

''What?'' Shock rippled down her spine.

''I called them after you collapsed. Took myself off the case.'' He raked fingers through his hair. ''I've hurt them, too. I had to tell them that I didn't know if you'd ever meet them now because of how I'd screwed up.'' He shook his head. ''Maddie didn't waste time yelling at me. She simply told me they'd be here in a few hours, whether or not you'd see them.''

He looked at Lacey. ''They've been waiting, hoping you'd want to meet them as much as they want to meet you. They care, Lacey. They're prepared to give you all the love and support you could ever want.''

''Just like that? Without even knowing me?''

''You're family.'' He shrugged. ''That's all they need to know.'' Dev watched her closely. ''So are you going to give them a chance? Are you ready to give yourself a chance?''

Ready? Would she ever be ready for this?

But how would she ever find her compass again if she didn't?

She squeezed her arms around her middle, but this time it was butterflies, not acid. ''I can't meet them here, not like this.'' She chewed a thumbnail. ''I don't know what to wear.''

She surprised a laugh from him. That quick and rakish grin she loved flashed across his face. ''You could wear a tow sack and they wouldn't care.''

"I don't think I have a tow sack. I don't think I've ever seen one."

"Oh, city girl, you've got some surprises in store. But Maddie was the consummate city girl herself when she first came. Boone can tell you stories...."

"You really like her, don't you?"

Dev nodded. "I like all of them, but Maddie especially. I just didn't register at the time that the reason was that she reminded me of you."

A tiny flare of joy lit within her. Maybe there was hope for them. "I'm frightened, Dev, but I want to do this."

His eyes...some kind of strong emotion peered out at her from them. There was so much left for them to deal with, and she didn't know how to handle any of it.

"Shh," he said. "I can see that brain clicking again. You'll be fine," he said, misunderstanding her worries. "You'll like them, too, I promise."

Her discussion with Dev should probably wait until after she filled in this huge hole in her past. "How soon can I leave here?"

"They'd be happy to come to the hospital."

"But I'm not meeting them in my old nightgown, Dev. Let's talk to the nurses. Dr. Byrne said I could go home when I was ready. Then Maddie and the others can come to my house, or I can go to them, whatever they prefer."

"Don't push yourself too hard. Maybe you should stay another night or two."

"I'm ready to go home."

Dev's brows pulled together. "We'll see what

the doctor says. You don't have any clothes in which to leave unless I bring them."

Then he walked out the door, infuriating and far too bossy.

But then Lacey smiled. Bossy and domineering, yes.

But not remote.

A few hours later, Lacey was home, showered and dressed after changing her clothes four times. She paced her bedroom, then darted back for one more look in the mirror.

Maybe not this long white knit sheath. Maybe the red sundress—

The same man who had picked her locks knocked at the door now. "You decent?"

She gnawed on her thumbnail. "Decent but dressed wrong."

He pushed the door open, then whistled softly. "You look beautiful to me." In his eyes she saw memories of that night...their night of magic.

She touched her fingers to her lips and wondered if they'd ever find their way back to that magic place.

"Stop worrying," he said softly. "Remember what the doctor said. No pressure on yourself." He crossed the room and held her shoulders. "There's no pressure from anyone else who's going to be here. Maddie cried when I called her, she was so happy."

"She did?" Lacey studied his eyes carefully.

He nodded. "She wants to love you, Lacey. That's all she wants. She's been alone before, too."

The doorbell rang, and Lacey's stomach gave a twist.

"Deep breath," Dev urged. "Then blow it all out in a gust. It'll relax you."

She tried to comply, but she could only manage a small, gulping breath.

Dev pulled her close and kissed her forehead. "It's going to be fine. And I'll be right here."

She tried not to read too much into it, but she was so very grateful. Her Margaret DeMille aplomb had utterly deserted her. "Thank you," she whispered.

He pulled away but kept her hand in his as he walked her toward the door.

Lacey walked beside him, frozen in fear and hope.

Dev felt how tightly Lacey was wound and knew a moment of real fear. There was too much on the line. If he was wrong and she hated the Gallaghers, everything she'd been through would be for nothing. Whatever tiny hope he might still harbor for a future with her would be out of the question because he would forever be a reminder of all that she had lost.

He knew Lacey well enough now to see that she couldn't go back to her old life, no matter how much she might wish for it. He didn't know how she would ever forgive him if this was a bust.

A part of him still wanted her to love the Gallaghers simply to make Charles DeMille suffer for all that his arrogance had inflicted on others. Another part of him recognized that what he'd been through had made Dev the man he was. He was strong, and he was a survivor. DeMille couldn't matter.

It was Lacey who was at risk now.

Lacey…and his own beat-up heart.

So close…they'd come so close to the dream he'd buried for years. But if they couldn't make it past this hurdle…if Lacey couldn't accept her past, he would forever be a reminder of pain, and whatever chance they might have would be finished.

So he tried not to think, and he opened the door.

She let go and stood behind him like a statue. He wanted to touch her so badly. Wanted to pull her into his arms and shield her.

But she only needed protection from her own fears. And from him. It wasn't these people who had hurt her.

"Dev!" Maddie bounded through the door and threw her arms around him. "Oh, Dev—" Her eyes were bright and filled with tears as she spotted her sister.

Lacey's eyes were huge in her face. Her very set, cold face. Dev wondered if only he saw that her knuckles were white where she gripped her hands together.

"Lacey DeMille, I'd like you to meet Maddie and Boone Gallagher—"

He never got a chance to finish. Maddie barreled right past that princess mask and threw her arms around the sister she'd waited so long to meet.

Lacey froze, and Dev moved closer, torn between protecting her and protecting Maddie's generous heart. But then, finally, he saw Lacey's hands rise and touch her sister's back gently.

Maddie hugged her hard, tears streaming down her cheeks. Then she stepped back. "Let me look at you—I'm sorry, I'm just so—" She turned to her husband. "Oh, Boone, she's here. Finally, finally, she's with us. Dev, I love you, I'm going to cook anything your heart desires, you just have to say the word—oh, look, we have the same eyes. Boone, she's got my eyes—"

Boone chuckled, but Dev saw a sheen in his eyes, too. He stepped closer and grabbed Maddie around the waist. "You're babbling, sweetheart. Give her a chance to take a breath," he said gently, squeezing Maddie's waist.

Maddie still held Lacey's hand as though she would never let go. Lacey looked poleaxed.

Boone was accustomed to gentling skittish horses. He sized Lacey up in an instant and took a different tack. His voice gentle and pitched low, he spoke to her. "Hello, Lacey. You must be tired. Would you like to sit down?"

Boone was a wizard with horses, and Dev could see Lacey respond to his calm voice. One look at her eyes told him Boone was right. She was both exhausted and stone-cold scared.

Lacey looked stricken. "I'm so sorry. I should offer you something to drink or—"

Boone grinned. "Don't feel bad. Maddie knocked me for a loop the first day I met her, and I haven't recovered yet." He leaned down and whispered. "But she's fairly harmless. Just watch out or she'll have you eating tofu and calling it something that sounds good."

A quick smile flitted across Lacey's lips. "I like tofu."

Maddie shot Boone a triumphant grin, then swooped close to hug Lacey again. "I promise I'll stop doing this as soon as I'm sure you're real." She turned them both toward the sofa, wrapping her arm around Lacey's waist, zooming past all the shyness just like Dev had foreseen. "You've been in the hospital. You sit down right here with me, and Dev can go get us something to drink, right, Dev? Boone, you'll help him? And then you'll bring the photo albums and Grandmother's diary?"

Boone turned to Dev and grinned. He pointed down the hall. "We've got our orders. This way?"

Dev glanced back, torn. But it wasn't his place now. His job was done. "Glad to see nothing's changed. Maddie's still ordering us all around like we were her wait staff."

Boone paused. "She'll thank you properly once she gets past being delirious." He stuck out his hand. "I'll thank you now." When they shook hands, Boone clapped his free hand on Dev's shoulder, and Dev saw the depth of the emotion Boone was trying to hide. "You've put a whole family back together."

Dev felt his own throat tighten. He headed for the kitchen. "Maddie's the agent of all this, her and Sam. I just did the footwork—not too damn well, as it turns out."

Boone looked sympathetic. "Want to talk about it?"

Dev glanced back at the two dark heads so close together. "Not really. Nothing to say."

Boone wasn't a man to pry, but he nudged just a little. "You said you'd known her before."

Dev shook his head and stared at the ground. "I should have told you how well. There's a lot of bad history between her family—her adoptive family," he corrected, "and mine."

"Anything we can do to help?"

"Nope. I'm not sure there's anything to be done."

"The way you look at her reminds me of something I used to see in the mirror."

Dev shot him a glance. "What's that?"

"A guy who's trying to convince himself he hasn't fallen like a ton of bricks for a woman he shouldn't want." Boone's blue eyes were full of humor and pity when he slapped Dev on the back. "I think I may enjoy watching this."

"Thanks a lot. After what you went through when you thought Maddie and I were having an affair, I guess you think it's funny."

"I should, but I don't. I remember only too well how it felt. You want to talk, I'll listen." He nodded toward the kitchen cabinets. "Let's get finished and rescue Lacey before Maddie completely bowls her over."

"I'm not sure I'm going to stay. This should be private."

Boone arched one eyebrow. "Never took you for a coward, Marlowe. Mitch and Perrie and Davey won't be here for another couple of hours. I'll have my hands full with Maddie and the tears she's gonna weep all over me. Lacey's yours to handle."

"Lacey's not mine." No matter how he wished she were.

"So you say," Boone said easily. "Buck up, Dev. A few tears won't kill you."

Even one more tear from Lacey would undo him, but Dev didn't say that. He opened the cabinet and handed Boone two glasses.

Hours later, they stood at the doorway saying goodbye. Boone had practically had to pry Maddie out bodily to get her to leave. They'd driven off, needing to get back to the ranch, but only after Lacey had promised to visit very soon. If Maddie could have figured out a way to do it, Dev had a feeling she would have packed Lacey up and taken her with them.

Lacey hugged Davey one more time. Tall, dark Mitch, ever the stoic, stood at the door. He spoke quietly, his dark eyes holding her. "I'd like it if you'd come to the wedding. I've been without family for a long time."

Tiny blond Perrie chimed in, leaning into Mitch's side. "I don't have any family at all besides Davey and the Gallaghers, and I've decided Maddie's not the only one who wants a sister. It would mean a lot to all of us if you'd come, Lacey." She leaned around Mitch and Lacey. "You'll bring her, Dev, won't you?"

He and Lacey had a lot of ground to cover before then. Right now, she looked so exhausted she was almost translucent. "I'll be there," he agreed. Whether Lacey would come was something he wouldn't predict. "You all drive safely."

"Bye, Dev. Bye, Aunt Lacey," Davey called.

Mitch nodded at Dev, brushed his hand gently over Lacey's hair, then herded his new family outside.

When Lacey closed the door and turned around, her eyes were awash with tears.

Dev's heart seized. "Come on," he said, taking her arm. "You're worn out. I'll clean up while you get ready for bed."

Lacey looked up at him. "I am exhausted, but oh, Dev, you were so right. They're wonderful. I couldn't have created a more beautiful family if I'd dreamed them up myself." She hugged her arms to her sides. "I can't sleep yet. I'm too wound up."

"Then at least come over here and sit down on the sofa."

She followed him without complaint, settling back into the cushions.

Between them, a strained silence fell.

Dev was as tired as he'd ever been. He'd had very little sleep since before the night of their date, which seemed a thousand years ago now.

Had they really experienced that night of bliss? His body told him yes. He'd wanted her then; he wanted her still. But that night lived across a huge chasm of painful emotion and distrust. Building a bridge would take effort, and Lacey's resources were stretched thin.

There was so much he wanted to know, so much he wanted to discuss—but he wasn't sure he wanted the answers he might hear. Instead he busied himself picking up glasses and plates.

"Dev—" Lacey's voice sounded odd.

He glanced up to see her studying him solemnly, her eyes huge and haunted.

"Want me to leave?" he asked.

Confusion filled her gaze. Then she shook her head and looked away from him.

After a moment, she drew in a deep breath and turned back, pulled her arms into herself as if for protection. "Tell me, Dev. Tell me what he did."

He knew she meant her father. "Not now. When you're better, but not now."

"I have to understand. I have to know why. I have to figure out who I am, where I belong. I need to know who this man who calls himself my father really is. Please. If you care at all about me, tell me."

Oh, I care, all right. Too damn much.

"I don't think you're up to it right now."

For a second, her eyes sparked. "You have no right to decide for me anymore. No one does. I've learned that one thing from all of you making decisions about my life. I guess I should thank you— you've freed me not to care what you think I'm ready to handle."

Touché. Dev nodded. "All right." He set down the dishes, shoved his hands in his pockets and began to pace, trying to think how best to say it.

Lacey tensed, but she had to hear this, no matter what it was. They couldn't go forward without her understanding the missing pieces of the puzzle.

"He framed my father."

Lacey couldn't stifle her gasp.

Dev glanced at her, then went on. "My father was a good man. An honest man. We never—" He glanced away. "We could never understand, never believe that it was true what they said about him."

His eyes locked on hers again. "He made some mistakes. My mother liked pretty things. Liked going places. She was a beautiful woman, and you knew, just watching them, that he would give her the world if she asked."

"That sounds very romantic." Not at all like her mother's—like Margaret's stiff propriety. She could never even imagine her parents kissing. She'd never seen it, not once.

"He worked for your father, did you know that?"

Shocked, she shook her head. Then she felt subtly ashamed. She'd never thought about where Dev had come from before he'd appeared in her life. Those magical weeks when they'd been so young, she hadn't cared. She only knew that he was exciting, that he made the world sparkle, made her blood run hot. Made her feel so very alive. "What did he do?"

"He was a junior partner on the rise. Then the economy fell apart in Houston and accountants were being laid off right and left." His thumb rubbed absently over his jaw. "I didn't know a lot of this until after the night—" he shot her a glance "—the night you and I—"

He looked away, seemed to gather himself. "One day our lives were fine. Camps and toys and the new car he'd promised me when I could drive. Then everything changed."

"How old were you?"

"Fifteen."

So young. She ached for that boy.

"Things hadn't been all good. Dad worked long hours and was tired all the time. I could tell he was under pressure, but all I really worried about was how soon I'd get to drive—" His voice went tight. "I should have seen. Should have known something was wrong."

"No one pays much attention to anything but themselves at that age."

But Dev wasn't buying. "I was the oldest. He always told me he knew he could count on me if anything ever happened."

Something had. She didn't know what, but she could see the strain of it on his face.

"One day he came home early. Too early. I heard my mother crying. Saw him sit outside in the dark for hours." Dev looked up at her then, and his eyes were dark holes of anguish. "I didn't go outside. I didn't know what to say, what to do. I'd never seen him look defeated like that."

"You were only a boy, Dev."

He faced the window, jamming his hands in his pockets and looking outside, his face all stark angles and lonely shadows. "Sometime in the night, he died." She saw a muscle flex in his jaw. A shudder ran through his frame. "I never knew he had a history of heart problems."

"You couldn't have done anything." You were just a boy, she thought, and her heart twisted.

When he turned to face her, his eyes were hot and angry. "It was the disgrace that killed him. He'd been indicted for fraud." His nostrils flared. "Everything he did, he did because Charles De-

Mille forced him to do it. It was the price of keeping his job. Your father promised that no one would ever find out, but when the heat came down, my father was the sacrificial lamb.''

"I'm so sorry, Dev. I don't—no wonder you hate him.''

"That's not all he did, Lacey. Maybe you don't want to hear.''

She didn't. But she would. "Tell me.''

"I tried to be the man of the house, to take care of all of them like my dad had asked. But he'd canceled all but one tiny insurance policy, and their lifestyle—our lifestyle—had drained any savings. Overnight, everything changed. We had to move into this dinky little nothing house, and the newspapers had been full of the scandal. Our name was ruined. There was nowhere to go that people didn't whisper. Our so-called friends vanished. And my mother started drinking. She couldn't handle it—or the kids.''

"Oh, Dev—'' Lacey grieved for the boy who'd tried to take all of that on his shoulders. "You were so young.''

He whirled on her, agitation filling his frame. "I tried to handle it—I *was* handling it. Maybe not like we were used to, but I was doing the best I could. Then your father comes sweeping in and makes my mother think he's some kind of savior. He brushed me aside like I was nothing. That's what he told me I was—nothing. Just a kid. He would make it all better.''

The bitterness still lingered in his voice. She could feel a proud teenager's impotent fury. She had no idea what to say, so she remained quiet, wishing she could think more clearly, wishing she knew what to do.

Then Dev laughed. It hurt her ears to hear it.

"He had a hell of a lot of nerve, I'll hand him that. Tear our lives apart with one hand, dispense charity with the other. He must have had a real laugh." His jaw worked as he ground out the words. "I got into a brawl one night and got arrested. My mother called him to help and he came and bailed me out. I didn't want his money. I forced him to let me work it off." His eyes turned haunted, brilliant green dulled. "And that's how I met you."

The air in the room was charged with memory.

"Worse luck for you," he murmured. His gaze went fierce. "It's like I told you—it was about revenge then. I wanted to hurt him, and I didn't care how it happened. You were a means to an end."

His voice went hoarse, dropped almost to a whisper. "You deserve to hate me. It doesn't matter that I fell in love with you, that I never meant to hurt you. I did hurt you, and you're still suffering for my actions."

Dev turned away, moved to the door, agitation in every line of his frame. "There is no reason for you to forgive me—for then or for now. I made the wrong choices, and you paid the price." His voice lowered. "Tell me who you want to come stay with you and I'll call them. I think I should leave."

He waited for what seemed forever, his hand gripping the door handle. Finally, he heard a soft sob. He squeezed his eyes shut. Then he heard her.

"No." Softly. Barely a whisper.

Dev turned. Haunted gray eyes lifted to his. Lacey shook her head, her voice full of tears when she answered. "There's no one else I want."

She studied him sadly. "I'm sorry I didn't fight for you back then. I'm sorry I didn't stand up to him when you asked me to go with you. If it's any consolation, I never got over you."

Afraid to hope, still he took a step toward her.

Lacey held up her hand to stop him. "I'm not much of a bargain, Dev. There's a lot I don't know." She swallowed hard. "I don't know how to feel about what my parents—what Charles and Margaret did. I don't think I can live the way I have anymore or accept what I thought was mine, but I don't know how to support myself or what I'm any good at doing."

He saw resolve forming on her face. "But I have figured out that no one can decide any of that but me." She reached toward him, then pulled her hand back. "One thing I already know is that you've paid as dearly as I have—probably more. I lived my life in the lap of luxury. I might not have felt like I fit, but I never once went hungry or had to think about taking care of anyone but myself."

He closed the distance between them. "You were young and sheltered. I understand."

She held herself away. "Do you? You shouldn't. After what they did to you—"

Dev shook his head. "It's over. What's done is done. If there's one thing I've learned it's that the past can choke you."

He caressed her jaw with fingers that weren't quite steady. "I never meant to hurt you when I came back.'' His voice tightened. ''I am so damn sorry—I swear to you it wasn't about revenge, not this time. I just didn't know how to tell you the right way that you're adopted. I knew it was going to tear your world apart, so I didn't trust anyone else to do it—but then I put it off, telling myself that if I spent some time with you, I'd figure out the magic words.''

Her eyes studied him so solemnly. He didn't know if he could ever make her understand.

''I tried to tell myself it was just a job, that it wasn't personal.'' He snorted softly at himself. ''That delusion lasted about two seconds after I saw you again.''

Touching her chin gently, he tilted it up. ''It's personal, Lacey. It's important. *You're* important. I played it wrong, and you paid. I thought that if we could have some time together before I told you, maybe I wouldn't have to lose you again. But I was wrong to do that. Selfish as hell. I just—''

Dev saw the tears shimmering in her eyes and knew he had to say it, had to try, even if he lost big. ''I don't deserve you, but I love you. More than my life, more than my honor, more than any hope of justice.''

Lacey's fingers covered her lips as tears spilled over her lashes. He thought he'd sell his soul to know what she was thinking. But whatever it was, he had to give her a way to find her peace with both families. If he could do that, then even if he lost her, she could go forward and build her new life. But he wasn't conceding her yet.

''I want us to get past this, to see if there's a

chance for us. I don't need revenge—I need you.
What's been done to me can't be changed. I am
who I am because of what I went through. If the
man I am could be good enough for the princess,
then everything that has happened would be worthwhile.''

"I'm not a princess," she whispered.

"You are to me." Dev clasped both of her hands
in his, holding them against his chest. "Is there a
place for me in this new life of yours, Lacey?"

Heart in his throat, he waited for her answer.

Her fingers gripped his. "I've waited all my life
for you, Dev. Since I was sixteen years old, every
man I've known has been measured against you."

Deep inside Dev, a dark ache eased and hope
flickered.

Then her eyes turned sad. "But I still have a lot
to figure out and maybe you don't want—" She
started to move away.

"I want," Dev growled, pulling her tightly into
his body with shocking suddenness. "You have no
idea how I want—"

He covered her mouth with a kiss so hot, so pos-
sessive, that Lacey melted against him. Her
thoughts evaporated in the heat and sweetness that
suffused her every pore. Soon she was twining her
arms around him, trying to get closer, feeling again
the hunger of their night to remember, the night of
magic.

Dev lifted her into his arms and strode toward
the bedroom. He ended a scorching kiss, his voice
fierce. "I want *you*. The real Lacey, not her money,
not her fancy address. The girl who climbed down

a trellis with me and the woman she's become.'' Those brilliant green eyes singed down to her soul.

For a moment, time seemed to stop, and she savored it, realizing that her whole life had just changed, her whole world just shifted. Part of her wanted the world to freeze so that she could live in this moment forever.

Part of her was eager to see what came next.

Then Dev lowered her to lavender silk, holding her close as he followed her down, settling his hard body over hers, his eyes naked as they'd once been in a moonlit gazebo.

''I love you, Dev.'' She'd waited a lifetime to say the words.

So close. Dev shuddered as the realization battered. He'd come so close to losing her, yet by some miracle he'd escaped with a second chance.

''I love you, too.'' His throat seized. ''You, Lacey, the real you. For always.''

''We're going to make it this time, aren't we?'' Her eyes were huge and luminous as moonlight shifted over their bodies.

His answer was a vow dragged up from the bedrock of his soul. ''If I have to battle the devil himself, nothing is ever going to part us again. No one, Lacey. Believe that. I'm so damn grateful that—'' His voice turned rough. He didn't have the words he needed to tell her how deep inside him she lived.

Lacey brushed her fingers over his beloved face, her once-empty heart full to bursting. ''I believe you. Oh, Dev...I need you so. I've missed you for so long.''

She pressed herself against him and for a moment, they simply clung.

Bereft of words, Dev decided to let his body speak for him, his touch tell her that she was...everything. With more care than ever, Dev bent to savor her, the taste of her, the silk of her skin. He couldn't get enough. Would never get enough of her.

And Lacey gave herself up to the man who'd given her the dream, who had seen past the surface down to her most vulnerable self—and loved her anyway.

She shivered as his mouth branded her skin. She'd been so hollowed out. So lost. Now she had so much.

A family, brothers and sister.

A man to love, the man of her dreams.

Then Dev's magical hands and restless mouth deprived her of thought. Gentleness vanished beneath a warrior's possession, a sorcerer's touch. Madness seized them both, fierce in its wonder.

With a sigh of relief, Lacey let go of decorum, cast away polite manners. The princess climbed down the trellis from her prison.

Waiting below was a daredevil knight on a black charger, his green eyes hot with power and passion.

The real Lacey jumped, knowing that Dev would always catch her.

Epilogue

From the front of the old country church, Dev watched Lacey walk down the aisle first, Maddie following her as matron of honor at Mitch and Perrie's wedding.

Lacey caught his eye and winked, and Dev winked back, his heart soaring. He would never get tired of this new Lacey who laughed so freely, who was learning to tease and play. When she slid her tongue across those lush lips while staring straight at him, it was all Dev could do not to stride across the church and grab her right now—and to blazes with anyone who might protest.

Then she reached the front and took her place as Perrie's bridesmaid, her brothers blocking his view. Dev shifted to the left, to find her still watching him.

She winked again, her eyes full of promise.

Dev grinned.

Then Boone stirred in front of him, and Dev turned his head to watch Maddie come down the aisle. She only had eyes for Boone, a secret smile playing between the two of them. Only last night, they had shared the news that they would be parents in seven months. A new life to heal the pain of the past, the blood of Dalton and Jenny uniting in joy and celebration this time around.

Then Perrie appeared in the doorway, a vision in Jenny Gallagher's wedding gown, her eyes fixed on Mitch and glowing with love. Davey proudly held her arm, all set to give her away. Mitch went very still, his dark eyes fastened on her and the small blond boy who already called him Dad.

Dev stood as groomsman behind Mitch and Boone, thinking how much life could change. A year ago, he'd never heard of any of the Gallaghers. Now one man and wife had come together from the ashes of tragedy and heartache; after today there would be two couples.

Dev intended to make it three as soon as possible.

Only one shadow remained—Lacey's relationship with the DeMilles. She would never fully heal until she dealt with them. Dev felt a faint tug of nerves, hoping that his surprise didn't blow up in his face.

Then the ceremony started, and Dev forced himself to concentrate.

Lacey stroked Davey's hair at the reception on the lawn of Boone and Maddie's two-story dream of a house. She'd loved it on sight, this place of her roots. "You were very dignified, Davey. And you look so handsome in your suit."

The five-year-old grinned, then motioned her to lean down. "I was kinda nervous, Aunt Lacey. Don't tell anybody, okay?"

Aunt Lacey. She couldn't get over how wonderful it sounded. "Okay," Lacey stage-whispered back, hugging him. She couldn't wait to bring Christina to meet him. Then he scampered off to find his adored Mitch, and she looked around to see where Dev had gone.

Maddie appeared at her elbow, touching her lightly on the back. Lacey glanced over as Mitch and Perrie walked up to her other side, Davey in tow, and Boone moved toward them across the grass. They arranged themselves around her silently like a protective flank, expectation buzzing through the air.

Then Dev appeared before her, looking serious. She frowned slightly, wondering. He leaned close and murmured, "Do you trust me, sweetheart?"

"Yes, of course. Dev, is something wrong?"

Dev stepped away from in front of her. Lacey saw her parents approaching, looking uncertain in a way she'd never seen them before.

Lacey watched her mother's eyes fill with tears she'd thought she would never see Margaret

DeMille shed. She saw her father, looking much older, study Dev for a long moment.

The silence felt stilted. Awkward.

Her mother spoke first. "Darling, we're so sorry. It was misplaced pride that kept us silent. You were ours from the first moment, you were a treasure we never thought to find. We didn't want anyone to have a claim on you, but we should have told you. You have to know that you've been a joy to us for all these years, and if you leave us now—" Her mother choked up.

Charles DeMille took over. Voice slightly hoarse, he looked straight at Lacey. "Princess, what I did to keep you and Devlin apart was because I thought I knew what was best for you." He cleared his throat. "I told Devlin that he was nothing, that he would never be good enough for my daughter. I was wrong. I know that now."

He glanced at Dev. "I will have to live with the knowledge of what I did to the Marlowes in the name of keeping a business going. That won't be easy, but neither will what he has offered be easy for him. He doesn't want our past battles to tear you apart, so he's informed us that he is not going to pursue the matter." Charles shook his head. "The man cares enough for you to give up his chance for justice in order to spare you. If I ever needed proof of how wrong I was about him…"

Her father's shoulders settled into resignation. "I still intend to do what I can to make it up to his family, but the only price he has asked is that we not make you choose between your two families. He seems to think that you still need us in your life, that you can forgive us.'' He paused, then looked at her, bereft of his usual certainty. ''Is he right?''

''Oh, Daddy—'' Stunned and shaky, Lacey looked up at Dev, leaning into his side, feeling his support and strength. After what her father had done to him, Dev deserved better.

''Lacey, it's all right,'' Dev murmured, his green eyes soft and concerned. ''I'll be all right. You need this.''

It was true—she couldn't live in this state of armed truce. It was the shadow that hung over all that was so good in her life now.

She looked around her at the new faces she already loved—bighearted Maddie, strong, gentle Boone, solemn, steady Mitch, sweet Perrie and adorable Davey. They all smiled at her as if giving her their blessing.

She faced her parents and took an uneven breath. ''Dev's right. I don't want it to be this way. I don't want to let the past cloud the future anymore.'' She swallowed hard. ''I love you both very much. If you can accept my new family, I'd like us to start again and build a new future, all together.''

With a cry, her mother reached out. Lacey moved into their arms, hugging them both, feeling peace sweep over her.

Then from the porch of the two-story white house both Dalton and Jenny had loved, Lacey heard a song begin to play. When she realized what it was, she turned back to Dev.

He grinned, and memories of a night she'd never forget washed over her.

"They're playing our song, sweetheart." He held out a hand.

She swallowed back tears and went into his arms. "Oh, Dev. What you've given me—"

He held her close. She snuggled against him, wanting never to leave. Then he pulled away gently and looked down into her face, stroking her cheek.

"It was a selfish move on my part, getting everyone you love together in one place." Dev grasped her hand, then dropped to one knee before her. He reached in his pocket and withdrew a small square box. "This comes a lot of years later than it should have, but not too late, I hope."

Then his eyes grew very serious. "Lacey, will you do me the honor of becoming mine for the rest of my life? Will you build a family with me, starting with Christina?"

Tears flooded her eyes. She glanced quickly around her at all the dear faces, then she fixed her gaze on the only man she would ever love.

"Oh, Dev, I never want to be apart from you again." She smiled through her tears. "I'd love to marry you. Just say when."

"Would after this dance be too soon?" Dev grinned, those devil's green eyes sparkling. "Quick—somebody bring back the minister."

There was laughter at his teasing, but Lacey saw tears and heard a few sniffs.

Dev rose and slipped the ring on her finger, gazing down into the silvery eyes that had bewitched him so many years ago and always would.

"Dance with me, my love." He pressed a kiss to the hand that bore his ring. Never taking his gaze from her, lest this dream vanish as had a young man's dreams so long ago, he swept her onto the dance floor.

Eyes locked on one another, they danced to the strains of the song that described who she was to him, who she'd always been.

His past. His present. His future.

His forever.

"My Girl."

* * * * *

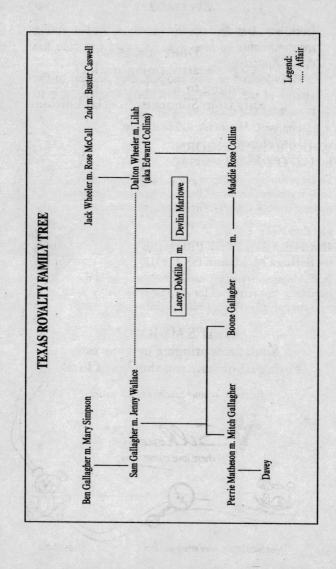

TEXAS ROYALTY FAMILY TREE

Ben Gallagher m. Mary Simpson

Sam Gallagher m. Jenny Wallace

Jack Wheeler m. Rose McCall   2nd m. Buster Caswell

Dalton Wheeler m. Lilah
(aka Edward Collins)

Lacey DeMille   m.   Devlin Marlowe

Boone Gallagher   ———   m.   ———   Maddie Rose Collins

Perrie Matheson m. Mitch Gallagher

Davey

Legend:
..... Affair

Don't miss
an exciting opportunity
to save on the purchase of
Harlequin and Silhouette books!

Buy any two Harlequin or
Silhouette books and save
$10.00 off future Harlequin
and Silhouette purchases

OR

buy any three
Harlequin or Silhouette books
and save **$20.00 off** future
Harlequin and Silhouette purchases.

*Watch for details
coming in October 2000!*

PHQ400

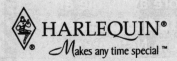

If you enjoyed what you just read,
then we've got an offer you can't resist!

Take 2 bestselling
love stories FREE!
Plus get a FREE surprise gift!

MONTANA MAVERICKS

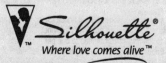

WED IN WHITEHORN

The legend lives on...as bold as before!

MM

Coming in September...

THE MARRIAGE BARGAIN

by

VICTORIA PADE

Corporate raider Adam Benson vowed to bring down the man he blamed for his family's ruin. And what better way to start than by marrying his enemy's daughter? But he hadn't planned on falling for his own prisoner....

MONTANA MAVERICKS:
WED IN WHITEHORN continues with
BIG SKY LAWMAN by **Marilyn Pappano**,
available in October from Silhouette Books.

Available at your favorite retail outlet.

Silhouette®

SPECIAL EDITION™®

COMING NEXT MONTH

#1345 THE M.D. SHE *HAD* TO MARRY—Christine Rimmer
Conveniently Yours
Lacey Bravo wasn't marrying a man just because she was in the
family way.... She was holding out for true love. And that meant
Dr. Logan Severance had to do more than propose. He had to prove he
was offering the real thing—his heart!

#1346 FATHER MOST WANTED—Marie Ferrarella
Being in the witness protection program meant not letting anyone get
too close. And that had been fine with Tyler Breckinridge—until his
three little girls led him to Brooke Carmichael, a woman whose
sweet temptations were breaking down his barriers and driving him
to distraction....

#1347 GRAY WOLF'S WOMAN—Peggy Webb
Lucas Gray Wolf wasn't about to let Mandy Belinda walk out of his
life. For she was carrying something that belonged to him—*his twins*.
But the red-hot passion this handsome loner felt for Mandy made him
want to claim more than his babies. He wanted to claim his woman!

#1348 FOR HIS LITTLE GIRL—Lucy Gordon
An unexpected turn of events had the beleaguered Pippa Davis
returning to Luke Danton—the man she'd loved but left behind. He
was the only one she'd trust to raise their daughter. Was his
undeniable connection to this beloved woman and child enough to
turn a bachelor into a devoted daddy?

#1349 A CHILD ON THE WAY—Janis Reams Hudson
Wilders of Wyatt County
Who was the delicate and pregnant beauty Jack Wilder rescued from
the blizzard? Lisa Hampton was a mystery to him—a mystery he
desperately wanted to solve. But would helping her recover the past
mean sacrificing his hope for their future?

#1350 AT THE HEART'S COMMAND—Patricia McLinn
A Place Called Home
With one sudden—*steamy*—kiss, Colonel John Griffin's pent-up
desire for Ellyn Sinclair came flooding back. His steely self-restraint
melted away whenever he was in Ellyn's irresistible presence. But
could a life-hardened Grif obey his heart's command?

CMN0800